THE PERFECT ROOMMATE

OTHER TITLES BY MINKA KENT

The Memory Watcher

The Perfect Roommate

The Thinnest Air

The Silent Woman

The Stillwater Girls

You Have to Believe Me

The Trophy Wife

When I Was You

The Watcher Girl

Unmissing

Gone Again

Dangerous Strangers Thrillers

Imaginary Strangers

THE PERFECT ROOMMATE

A THRILLER

MINKA KENT

This is a work of fiction. Names, characters, organizations, places, events, and incidents are either products of the author's imagination or are used fictitiously. Otherwise, any resemblance to actual persons, living or dead, is purely coincidental.

Text copyright © 2018, 2025 by Nom de Plume, LLC
All rights reserved.

No part of this book may be reproduced, or stored in a retrieval system, or transmitted in any form or by any means, electronic, mechanical, photocopying, recording, or otherwise, without express written permission of the publisher.

Published by Thomas & Mercer, Seattle

www.apub.com

Amazon, the Amazon logo, and Thomas & Mercer are trademarks of Amazon.com, Inc., or its affiliates.

EU product safety contact:
Amazon Media EU S. à r.l.
38, avenue John F. Kennedy, L-1855 Luxembourg
amazonpublishing-gpsr@amazon.com

ISBN-13: 9781662531606 (paperback)
ISBN-13: 9781662531590 (digital)

Cover design by Jarrod Taylor
Cover Image © MirageC / Getty; © Anton Starikov / Shutterstock

Printed in the United States of America

This one's for HJ—a most perfect friend.

PROLOGUE

All I needed was a cheap room to rent.
 I didn't plan this. I swear.

1

It's a pretty little house with an ugly little address.

47 Magpie Drive.

What should have been an ordinary Sunday kicked off with an eviction notice on my door and ended with my belongings shoved into wrinkled grocery sacks and the neighbor's stolen Wi-Fi on my computer. With just minutes to spare, I managed to find the perfect place—one that didn't require credit checks, a huge deposit, or a long lease.

With clammy palms stuck to the peeling steering wheel of my '97 Civic, I stare through my cracked windshield at an adorable whitewashed brick ranch nestled in the heart of a family-friendly neighborhood south of Meyer State's picturesque campus.

I find it difficult to believe that a college student lives here, but her ad was posted on the Tiger Paw Portal and a quick reverse search of her email address in the student directory revealed her name to be Lauren Wiedenfeld, senior in English lit.

Just like me.

In fact, I recognized her photo immediately, having taken a good handful of classes with her over the years. Shiny ash-blonde hair. Dimpled smile. Crystalline eyes accented by thick, curled lashes. I couldn't count how many times I'd seen her stare past me like I was invisible.

Just like everyone else.

Sniffing my shirt, I'm relieved to drag the scent of dollar store fabric softener into my lungs. I was in such a hurry on my way out, I wasn't sure if the clothes I'd grabbed were from the clean basket or not.

I need this girl to like me. If she doesn't? I'm not sure where I'll go. Apartments in this town come at a premium, and if it weren't for the fact that my car needed new tires and a new transmission this winter, I might still be holed up in my studio right now. Un-homeless.

Killing my engine, I shove the keys in my purse and check my reflection in the rearview.

At least I got to shower today. My hair is clean, my teeth are brushed, and my pits are slicked with two layers of store-brand deodorant. Plus, I don't reek of stale alcohol—which is more than most students around here can say on the weekends.

My hands threaten to tremble as I climb out of my car, and I try not to slam the door—I don't want to seem careless. The ground wobbles beneath my feet. If I were a superhero, social awkwardness would be my power. My entire life, I've struggled to get out of my head, constantly overanalyzing every little word or movement or shift of a gaze. I've learned it's easier to sit back and shut up. I find I don't make as much of a fool out of myself that way. Quietude has become the law of my land, with silence being my official language.

But I don't have a choice today.

If I want Lauren to welcome me with open arms as her shiny new roommate, I have to plaster a smile on my face, see her bubbly personality, and raise her one of my own.

After rapping on the front door a moment later, I wait with my arms straight at my sides. Signature awkwardness. My heart knocks in my chest before whooshing in my ears, and warmth blooms in my cheeks.

I haven't officially met her and already I'm blushing.

Shit.

Inhaling a breath of frosty February air, I soften my expression, loosen my shoulders, and wrap my right hand around the worn leather strap of my purse. I'm not sure if this is what casual and confident looks like, but the sound of the door latch tells me I don't have another second to try to figure it out.

"You must be Meadow?" I'm not sure what I was expecting, but Lauren is all smiles as she gets the door—as if she's *happy* to see me. "Come in!"

The scent of soft gardenia emanates off a flickering boutique candle centered on her glass coffee table, and in the corner, the glow of diffused lamplight paints the room in a welcoming ambience. Her phone is docked on a set of speakers next to her TV, playing the kind of chill music I'd expect to hear in some upscale Manhattan bar.

"Have a seat wherever you'd like," she says, lowering herself into a rattan chair covered in a faux fur throw. Lauren tucks her mile-long legs beneath her and adjusts her sweatshirt so it hangs just so, revealing a hint of her left shoulder. Her hair is piled on top of her head, and I'm convinced she's one of only ten people on the planet who can make a messy mane look chic.

Glancing around before I settle in the middle of her gray linen sofa, I have to remind myself to talk. "Love your place. So cute."

I can do this. I can be friendly even if I have to fake it. People like her don't understand people like me—the quiet type. They think we're weird. And no one wants to live with a weirdo.

Lauren's face lights but she shrugs, almost as if the flattery makes her uncomfortable. "Thanks."

"Is that your major? Interior design?" No way in hell I'm going to tell her I did a little research on her before I came here.

She shakes her head. "English lit. What about you?"

"Same." I exhale, sinking into the cushions. She's easier to talk to than I assumed she'd be. "I think we might have some classes together? I swear I've seen you in World Lit."

Lauren laughs, rolling her eyes. "No kidding? I'm so oblivious most of the time."

Of course.

That's why she looked through me all those times . . .

I'm still not sure if I'm buying this cutesy, friendly shtick of hers because girls like her can be sickeningly fake when they want to be, but I'm willing to give her a shot if she's willing to take a chance on me.

Besides, it's not like I have any other options to fall back on.

"People probably think I'm some snob." She waves her hand, endearing almost. "But I'm just in my own little world most of the time."

I pride myself on my keen observational skills, something I've honed and polished to sheer perfection over the years . . . but I may have been wrong about this one.

Maybe.

"You thirsty?" Lauren rises from her chair, straightening her shirt and eyeing the doorway to her kitchen. Since she's already up, I can't exactly say no. "FIJI water? San Pellegrino? Tea? I'd offer you a glass of wine, but it's only ten o'clock in the morning."

I chuckle out of politeness, not because I think she's funny. "Tap water is fine."

Her expression falls, as if she's unable to comprehend that my broke college student taste buds haven't yet acquired the taste of artisanal water. "Meadow, the lead levels in the water here are off the charts. Haven't you been following the news? It's all they're talking about anymore. And the city's broke. No plans to do anything about it. I'm telling you, Monarch Falls is going to be the next Flint, Michigan."

She disappears around the corner before I get the chance to tell her that between working twenty-four, sometimes thirty hours a week cleaning houses and taking sixteen credits, I don't exactly have time for late-breaking local news stories.

Lauren returns a moment later, a square bottle of luxury water in one hand and a floral-printed paper napkin in the other. She places them before me, like a proper hostess, and I can't help but wonder if she'll always be this formal once we live together.

If we live together.

This has to be an act.

People aren't actually this formal, are they? At least the ones back home, the ones I grew up around, weren't. I've never heard of anyone needing a coaster to go with their bottled water.

Then again, this coffee table looks pricey with its reclaimed wooden legs and crystal-clear glass top.

"Thanks." I take the water from her, unscrewing the cap and ensuring I don't so much as spill a drop.

This place is much too nice of a dwelling for a typical Meyer State student. Her family clearly comes from money.

I'll try not to resent her for that.

"So, tell me about yourself." Lauren settles into her chair again, resting her elbow on her knee and her chin on her hand, leaning toward me. My Intro to Psychology professor taught us years ago that when someone leans into you, they're interested, genuinely interested, in what you have to say. "What's your schedule like? Who's your ideal roommate? Do you smoke? Throw parties?"

Brows lifted, I let her questions marinate, unsure of where to begin. "Oh. Um. I don't smoke or drink. I don't party. So nothing to worry about there. I work. Part-time. And when I'm not working, I'm home. Usually studying. I don't make a lot of noise. Basically, I'm a clean-freak, studious homebody."

My cheeks flush and I feel myself growing flustered, but the fact that she isn't staring at me like I'm some kind of social reject is somewhat reassuring. I suppose I've never stopped to examine my uneventful existence, but I've always been content to keep to myself.

It's better if I don't know what I'm missing out on.

Lauren's face is lit as I ramble on, like I'm telling her everything she wants to hear.

"Okay, so what do you do for fun?" she asks.

I was hoping I could avoid that question. Pretty sure to someone like Lauren, I'm a shining example of a boring bookworm. Not the kind of person she'd be caught dead with.

"I like to see plays," I lie. I don't have money for a theater membership. Not even with the gracious 50 percent student discount. "And I see movies."

At the dollar theater. Maybe once every three months.

"Do you ever do Friday After Class at Wellman's?" she asks. "They have dollar wells from four to six."

Beer. Pass.

"Sometimes," I lie. Again.

Lauren sinks back, eyes still glued on me. "That place is always crazy packed. I bet we've been there at the same time and never even noticed."

Taking a sip of water, I nod. "I'm sure."

My tone echoes hers, something I do when I'm nervous. It's like second nature, adopting her body language, her intonations, the cadence of her words.

"Where do you work?" she asks.

I push a breath through my nostrils and roll my eyes. "Sparkle Shine Cleaning Co."

I hate that fucking name.

And the Minion-yellow car I'm forced to drive from client to client, the one that matches the Minion-yellow uniform I'm forced to clothe myself with.

But the pay is decent.

And it sure as hell beats working in food service. Food service means interacting with people all day long, being yelled at by customers when the kitchen screwed up their order or their fork has a water spot on it or I'm not refilling their third glass of Diet Coke fast enough.

No thanks.

"Never heard of it," Lauren says. "Do you like it?"

What kind of question is that? And what does she expect me to say? That I love scrubbing people's shit-stained toilets? Don't even get me started on some of the bathrooms I've had the pleasure of bleaching from floor to ceiling. Rich people—or people rich enough to pay someone to clean their house for them—aren't always as clean as one might expect.

I shrug and offer a tepid smile. "It's a job. What about you? Do you work?"

Lauren bites her lip and scrunches her face, hesitating for a second. "I don't."

Of course not.

"My parents want me to focus on my studies," she says, as if that makes up for her good fortune. "They said school should be my full-time job, so I get a monthly stipend as long as I keep my grades up. They did the same for my brother. They actually own this house. My brother lived here when he went to Meyer State and my younger sister will live here next year when she's a freshman. My parents didn't want to throw money away on rent, I guess. That's their excuse anyway. If you ask me, I think it's just a way for them to control their adult children."

She huffs. I huff.

"Anyway." Lauren shrugs, studying me, perhaps silently waiting for me to judge her. I keep a poker face.

"So what happened to the roommate before me?" I ask.

"I've never had one."

"Okay. So, why now?"

Exhaling, Lauren says, "So that stipend? It's based on my GPA. Last semester, I kind of got a little . . . distracted . . . and I failed a class. First time in my life. It was a seven AM on the north side of campus on Friday mornings. Anyway. It's no excuse. I failed it. GPA plunged. Parents were livid. Chopped my stipend in half—essentially barring me from having fun. Their way of punishing their twenty-three-year-old daughter."

"Oh." Nice to know I'm scrubbing toilets so she can get wasted with her friends.

This explains everything. The lack of a deposit, the lack of a lease, no background check. She's desperate for some supplemental income, willing to take in a stranger to maintain her cushy little life.

"Just to let you know . . . my parents won't know you're living here," she's quick to add. "And you'll only be able to stay through May. Maybe July. Depends on how quickly I land a job after graduation. I hope that works?"

So, she likes me.

She's *choosing* me.

Just like that.

"That's perfect actually," I say. "I'm graduating, too. Hoping to get the hell out of here."

I wear a smile that matches hers and we bask in a moment of mutual understanding for a single, endless second. Our desire to leave Monarch Falls might be the only thing we have in common, but I'll take it.

"You want me to show you around?" Lauren rises from her seat and straightens the hem of her top.

Returning my water to its floral napkin resting place, I stand. "Sure."

Spinning on the ball of her foot, she struts across the small living room, toward a dark hallway. I follow. Flicking on the light, she says, "This house is, like, a million years old. It's really dark. Windows are small. And your room is on the smaller side, by the way."

My room.

"I mean, the room you'd be renting," she clarifies. "If you want it."

Stopping at the last door, she reaches her hand inside and gets the switch.

Clearly we have different definitions of "small." This room is easily the size of my last apartment, complete with shiny wood floors, a double bed, a nightstand, a dresser, and two curtain-covered windows.

"But you'd get your own bathroom—the hall bath." Lauren's words are rushed, as if she's worried I'm having second thoughts. "I never use it."

We step inside, and she shows me the closet, which is the smallest thing about this room. But it's fine. I don't have a lot.

"What do you think?" Lauren lifts her nails to her mouth, watching for my reaction. "It's yours if you want it."

"You sure?" I lift an eyebrow. We've known each other all of fifteen minutes, though I suppose living with strangers is kind of the college way.

"Oh, my God, are you serious?" She laughs. "You're everything, Meadow. All that stuff you told me? You're the *perfect* roommate. Quiet. Studious. Polite. You're a rarity in this town, do you know that?"

Yes. Well aware. And she's kind to say that. I let her earlier words echo in my mind. No one's ever called me perfect before—in any context.

It feels kind of . . . amazing.

As much as I try not to, I beam like an appeased idiot, my ego practically purring like a milk-fed kitten.

I know nothing about Lauren Wiedenfeld besides the fact that she treated me like a human being today, which maybe marks the first time in my collegiate history that anyone's ever tried to have an actual conversation with me about anything, the first time someone's ever been so engaged and interested.

She's not the mean girl I expected.

"When do you want to move in?" she asks, bouncing on her toes and clasping her hands across her chest like an excited schoolgirl anticipating a slumber party. Not that I would know anything about that. I didn't have friends in school. I just saw the way other girls would giggle and jump around Friday afternoons as they talked about the sleepover they'd been planning all week and whose mom was doing the picking up and whose mom was doing the dropping off.

"Is . . . now . . . okay?" I ask, exhaling. "My stuff is in my car. I moved out of my apartment a while back, and I've been staying at my mom's, commuting back and forth."

I have to lie if I want this place.

And I do. I want it so bad.

This house is adorable and clean and it smells like fresh flowers and it's decorated like a page out of a Serena & Lily catalog. It would be the nicest place I've ever lived in. Maybe the nicest place I'll *ever* live in.

"Yeah, of course." If Lauren doesn't believe me about the commuting thing, she does a good job of hiding it. "You want me to help?"

We head out of the room and down the hall, her messy bun bobbing as she walks, and she reaches up to tighten it—which of course makes it look even better.

"No, it's fine. I don't have much," I say, realizing I sound like someone who's been living out of their car for God knows how long. "I mean, most of my stuff is back at my mom's. I didn't bring any furniture because your ad said the place was furnished."

I bite my tongue to keep from rambling on and making a mountain out of my molehill of a lie. I hate lying. It feels unnatural, slimy. And I hate liars.

But desperate times and all of that.

I fully expect karma to bite me in the ass after all the little white lies I've told today.

"Right," Lauren says. "My mother had this place professionally decorated." She reaches for a magnifying glass resting on top of a curated stack of interior design books on a marble-topped console. The handle is painted navy blue, with little stripes of bone-colored stone. "They went with a California coastal theme," she continues. "My mom grew up in Orange County. Moved here to New York when she married my dad. I don't think she ever got used to living in the frozen plains. You should see their house. Looks like it's better suited to the beach in Malibu than in some gated neighborhood outside Albany."

Ooh. A "gated" neighborhood. How fancy.

That's the thing about rich people, they feel the need to insert these little details so casually in conversation, as if you've forgotten for a moment that they have money. It's a crutch, I think. A side effect of their insecurity. And it's a damn shame, too. Lauren could be that much more likable if only she didn't feel the need to word vomit her privileged upbringing into every topic of conversation.

It's almost as if she's worried I won't like her—which is hilarious. No one's ever cared if *I* liked *them*.

"Anyway, I'll let you get settled," she says, turning to face me when we reach the end of the hall. "If you need any help with anything, I'll be in my room."

I smile and nod. It's exhausting having to talk this much, having to smirk and laugh and be social and constantly engaged.

But at least it didn't kill me.

Lauren disappears into her room, leaving the door open a crack. Soft, downtempo music plays a second later, the glow of her expensive, featherlight laptop filling her dark room. The sliver of light is like the tiniest peek into her world, and I must admit I'm curious—though I'm not sure why.

Heading out to my Honda to grab my things, I realize that I've parked behind her shiny black Lexus. We'll have to talk parking spots and particulars later. But for now, I need to focus on getting these bags and bins out of my back seat and into my beautiful new place.

Lugging the first plastic tote in my arms a minute later, I return inside and trek down the hall to my well-appointed guest suite. As I drop it on the center of my bed, the top loosens and falls to the wooden floor with a plastic-y thump. Swiping it off the floor, I catch the hint of a white envelope sticking out from beneath the ruffled bed skirt.

Upon first glance, it appears to be an old bill of some kind, or maybe a credit card offer? The return address is too generic to tell. I place it on top of the chest in the corner with the intention of giving it to Lauren when my gaze falls on the name.

Emily Waterford.

I grab the envelope again, examining the address.

47 Magpie Drive.

And the date on the postage meter sticker.

December 17 of last year.

Only two months ago.

Lauren looked me in the eyes and told me she'd never had a roommate before, that her dire financial situation essentially began this semester.

Did she . . . lie?

God, I hope not. As hypocritical as it may be, if there's anything in this world I can't stand, it's being lied to. It's disrespectful, insulting. My tolerance for bullshit and everyday annoyances is higher than most, and keeping my mouth shut when something bothers me is what I do best, but being lied to drives me *insane*.

It's like they think I'm stupid. Or unworthy of the truth.

Folding the envelope, I tuck it into my purse. I'm going to have to do some digging as soon as I get settled. But for now, I need to concentrate on not being homeless.

2

Lauren raps on my door at half past eleven, just as I've finished hanging the last shirt in my new closet. Storage at my last place consisted of a broom closet with wire shelving that never seemed to stay in place, collapsing if I hung one too many shirts on the top rung.

About time I moved up in the world.

"Come in," I say, taking a seat on my bed.

A second later, she's standing in the doorway, her lithe body covered in pricey-looking jeans and a Breton boatneck sweater. The bun is gone, replaced now with loose waves that drape over her shoulders effortlessly.

"I'm meeting a friend for lunch in a few," she says. "You want to come with?"

For a second, I'm speechless, convinced she's talking to some imaginary person standing behind me.

No one has *ever* invited *me* for a casual girls' lunch.

"Come on, it'll be fun!" Lauren grins, sensing my hesitation before striding across the room and taking the spot next to me. "You'll love Tessa. And she wants to meet you."

My brows lift.

Is this real life?

"I promise she's the sweetest person you'll ever meet." Lauren continues to try to sell me on this.

"Why does she want to meet me?" I ask.

Lauren blinks. My question doesn't compute. And I suppose I get it. College is all about meeting new people, making connections—a mecca for social butterflies like her. These are the years when everyone is supposed to want to know everyone else, to network before we dip our toes into the real world. But casual dinners and drinks and parties and hangout sessions are a language I've never spoken.

"Unless you're busy," she rises, sliding her hands in her back pockets, expression fading. I don't want to offend her. And I sure as hell don't want her to think *I'm* the snob in this situation. I may be a lot of things, but I'm not that. "Or maybe you have other plans? We can rain check it."

My stomach rumbles. I haven't eaten since last night. And of course I have no other plans. I don't even have groceries.

Ignoring the anxious prickle of sweat forming beneath my arms, I try my damnedest to convince myself to go despite the fact that every part of me doesn't want to. I'd rather sit here, listen to some David Bowie, close my door, and get lost in my own little world.

I *love* my world.

But I can't be rude.

Not to my *roommate*, the girl I'm going to have to see day in and day out for the next three months. It's important that we have a good rapport. We don't have to be friends, but we should be cordial and this is the first step.

"Okay, sure." I force a smile that lights her face.

"*Yaaaay,*" she says, voice soft as she claps. What is it with girls soft-clapping anytime they get excited? This isn't the PGA tour. "Is sushi okay? We're thinking Taki downtown?"

Sushi? What kind of college student has a budget for *Taki*? Not to mention the thought of eating raw fish makes my stomach churn. I've always been convinced people only claim to like sushi because it sounds cool.

I nod, my mouth watering—but not from hunger. "Of course."

Lauren goes to leave, and I think of the envelope. And Emily Waterford. Then I catch a glimpse of myself in the dresser mirror. If I'm going to get *sushi* at *Taki* with *Lauren* and *Tessa,* I need to look halfway presentable.

"Give me a few minutes?" I drag my fingers through the sandy-blonde mop on my head, hoping a ponytail will suffice.

She gives me a thumbs-up. And then she's gone.

Yanking the dresser drawers, I search for my newest pair of jeans, a Christmas gift from my grandmother who was appalled this past Thanksgiving when I confessed I didn't own a single pair without frayed hems or holes in the crotch. Next, I pull a shirt from the closet. A button-down. Pink with flowers. Probably better suited for a fifty-year-old white-collar professional than a twenty-two-year-old college student. It's not trendy and it's the kind of thing Lauren would never be caught dead in, but it isn't stained or stretched, so it'll have to do.

Digging around inside one of my totes, I find my small Ziploc baggie of drugstore makeup. Most of it is old—my mascara nearly dried out and past its expiration, but it's all I have.

My hair is last, and the stubborn idiot in me attempts to do one of those messy bun things on the top of my head.

I fail.

Miserably.

Which only causes my heart to race to the point that the room begins to spin, my breath quickens, and a thin glaze of sweat forms across my brow.

Why did she have to invite me? Does she think we need to be friends just because we're living together? I'm perfectly fine with doing the whole two-ships-passing-in-the-night thing with the occasional "hello" or "good morning."

A Xanax would be a godsend right now, but unfortunately, I used my last one four days ago, when I had to give a presentation in my English Women Novelists class.

Brushing my hair back, I succumb to my hairstyling incompetence and secure it in a basic ponytail before giving myself a final once-over in the mirror.

My mind refuses to quiet, reminding me of how awkward I look, how much I'm going to stand out with the two of them, how much I hate sushi, and how much happier I'd be if I just stayed here.

But I've already committed.

The sound of a horn honking from the driveway is my indication that it's too late to back out, even if I wanted to.

"Oh, hey, she's here," Lauren calls from the living room.

Everything happens so fast: grabbing my stained, faded canvas bag, stepping haphazardly into my worn flats, heading out into the brisk air, climbing into the back of Tessa's little red Mercedes.

The car is toasty and my jeans slide across the buttery black leather with ease.

"Tessa, this is Meadow," Lauren says as she climbs up front and secures her seatbelt. "My new roomie."

The friend turns to me, shiny dark hair curtaining her face until she brushes it away. Her eyes are an exaggerated round shape and the color of honey, slightly close together, but there's no denying she's beautiful.

"So glad you could come with!" Tessa says.

She studies me and I can imagine all the things she's thinking right now, about my hair, my clothes, my slumped posture, my fidgeting hands. Of course, she doesn't *look* like she's judging me, but I know she is. Girls like her always do.

"Thanks for the invite," I manage to say, finding solace in the merciful expression on her face and wanting to believe it's genuine. I almost think she feels sorry for me, and maybe that's worse than judging me.

Judge me all you want, but I don't need your pity.

Every part of me wants to curl up inside myself. I can handle one-on-one chats, for the most part, but as soon as more people are added to the mix I grow quieter, requiring an insurmountable amount of strength to be social.

"Hope you like Taki," Tessa says in a singsong voice as she backs out of the drive. Once on the street, she presses a button on her steering wheel and some kind of weird music—the stuff Lauren listens to—begins to emanate from the sound system. The display in the front dash says it's ESTHERO—HALF A WORLD AWAY.

Fitting.

Lauren and Tessa talk each other's ears off up front. I'm just along for the ride, content to be an afterthought tucked away in the back. It's easier to be accidentally forgotten than to be a bona fide third wheel.

"Did you know that, Meadow?" Lauren turns toward me a few minutes later, brows meeting.

"I'm sorry, what?" Shit. I completely spaced out their conversation.

"About Professor Cutler?" she asks, referring to the English department's chair who happens to teach the class I have with Lauren on Wednesday afternoons.

"What happened?" I ask. "I didn't hear you. I'm sorry."

She twists her entire body around, expression fading. "He had a stroke last week."

My world stops spinning for a moment despite the fact that I never much cared for Cutler. He laughs at his own off-color jokes, takes weeks to respond to emails, and goes off on far too many irrelevant tangents—mostly sports related—during lecture, but this is unfortunate.

"They're replacing him with Bristowe the rest of the semester," Lauren adds.

Holy shit.

"Bristowe?" A smile curls my lips no matter how hard I try to fight it. Professor Reed Bristowe taught three of my classes last year plus spent one semester filling in when my academic adviser was on maternity leave. He's quite possibly one of the finest, most charismatic educators Meyer State has ever known. So humble, too. And if that wasn't enough, he's all dimples and dark hair and looking like he walked off the pages of a J.Crew fall/winter catalog with his tweed blazers, cognac loafers, thick-rimmed glasses, leather messenger bag, and slim-cut khakis.

"Have you had him before?" Lauren asks.

I nod. "A few times. You?"

"Yep." She turns to face the front, and the red letters of the Taki sign come into view a couple of blocks down the road. "He's actually my faculty mentor for my senior capstone."

Of course she would be that lucky.

I got stuck with Professor Margaret Blume, who should have retired at least thirty-two years ago but for whatever reason refuses. Our meetings typically consist of her shouting for me to speak up because she can't hear and end with her forgetting everything we talked about in the thirty minutes prior.

If she's the reason tenure shouldn't be a thing, Reed Bristowe is the reason it should. He's everything a professor should be. Attentive, articulate, and always available.

And his wife, Elisabeth? Equally amazing.

I would know.

I clean their house every Monday from eight to ten AM. But of course, I can't share that. Sparkle Shine Cleaning Co. has me under a strict nondisclosure agreement. I'd hate to lose the Bristowe account.

Or my job.

"We're here." Tessa slides us into a parking spot by the front door and kills the engine. "I'm dying for a spicy tuna roll."

Lauren and Tessa link arms, which is a thing that girls do that I've never understood, and I follow them inside. In a matter of minutes, we're seated in a cozy corner booth, sliding our jackets off and shoving our purses into the mix. My ratty canvas bag looks out of place next to their matching monogrammed totes. Story of my life. The only thing matching about us is our cheeks, flushed from our brief stint in the cold.

The two of them aren't even looking at the menu. They must come here often.

"Know what you want?" Tessa asks me as she reaches for one of the ice waters our server has just delivered.

No, I don't know what I want. We've been here all of twelve seconds.

"Oh. Um." I grab a menu and try not to panic. If I order miso soup and seaweed salad, Lauren's going to know I lied about liking sushi. And if I order sushi, I'm going to throw up.

So it comes to this.

"I'm going to run to the restroom quick," Lauren says, sliding out of the booth and leaving her bag with Tessa. "Would one of you order me a Taki roll and a salmon roll?"

"Yeah, babe," Tessa says. Her gaze drifts across the table. She's studying me again, which makes it difficult for me to concentrate on the task at hand . . . figuring out what the hell I'm going to order. "You don't like sushi, do you?"

Oh, she's astute, this one. Not ditzy and oblivious like Lauren.

"What?" My heart plummets. All the letters on the laminated pages begin to blur together, and the ones that don't aren't making any sense. I can't concentrate like this, under all of this pressure.

"It's okay," she assures me, half laughing. Her hand reaches across the table, covering mine. My body stiffens. It's weird to be touched by someone else. "I can tell when someone's just being polite. Order the Sunday roll. It's cooked."

Exhaling, I'm blanketed in relief. "I didn't want to be rude earlier."

She waves her hand, dismissing my sentiment. "*So* not a big deal."

A minute later the server stops by to grab our orders, and Tessa requests three mizuwari martinis before I can protest that I don't drink and if I did, I certainly wouldn't order a cocktail that costs a ridiculous fourteen dollars a glass.

Shit.

"How long have you and Lauren known each other?" I ask when Lauren returns. Can't help but feel I'm letting my guard down, if only by an inch. But it's for the greater good. This entire arrangement is going to be easier if I like them and they like me—if only on a basic acquaintance kind of level.

They exchange looks, like they're trying to communicate telepathically.

"Since freshman year, I think?" Lauren answers first.

"Sophomore," Tessa corrects her. "We met at Anthro. The store, not the class. I was working. She was shopping. Story of my life."

"Oh, stop." Lauren swipes at Tessa's shoulder and they laugh. "You worked there maybe three months." She turns to me. "Then she met Rich, her sugar daddy."

Tessa's jaw hangs and she faces me. "She's messing with you. I don't have a sugar daddy."

I don't know whether to laugh with them or sit here in silence until I determine where the hell this conversation is going. From the sound of it, I'd say there's some kind of inside joke happening that I'm obviously not a part of, which would make it even more awkward if I were to play along and pretend I find any of this amusing.

"My dad invented this app," she says, rolling her eyes like she's told the story a million times. "Sold it to Google a few years ago."

So that explains the flashy red Mercedes. Her family is stupid loaded. New money types.

Reaching for my water, I smile and nod and sip because I don't know what I'm supposed to say. Congratulations on being set for life? Nice? Cool? Good for you?

"It's the neatest story. Tell her, Tessa," Lauren says, nudging her friend. She turns to me. "It's so inspiring."

"My dad had lost his job a few years before that," she says. "He worked in IT at this call center and all their jobs were shipped overseas completely out of the blue. Our town is literally in Middle of Nowhere, South Dakota, and the best work he could find was the local lube and filter connected to the Conoco in the next town over. No one else would take him. Said he was too overqualified or some shit. Anyway, every night, he'd come home and teach himself coding. After a while, he built this app . . . someone at Google caught wind of it and made him an offer he couldn't refuse. He's been spoiling us rotten ever since."

"Aw," I say, looking at Tessa in a completely new light. She isn't some silver-spooned princess. She's someone I *might* actually be able to respect, even if I am the tiniest bit envious of her Cinderella story.

Her father sounds like a real stand-up guy. Nothing like mine.

My dad was a small-town prick who peaked in high school and bailed when I was six after meeting some homewrecker in an AOL chat room. I spent the years that followed hating that unfaithful bastard. Mom spent the years that followed going through boyfriends the way girls like Lauren go through shoes, switching them out with the seasons, occasionally getting attached to a particular pair, and keeping them until the soles have worn and it's time to replace them all over again.

Her newest bedfellow is a contractor named Bug.

Not Bud. Not Buzz.

Bug.

As in the disgusting things that splatter on windshields and leave their guts everywhere.

Supposedly his real name is Conrad Sterling Pierce III. No joke. A name like that belongs to royalty or some Southern, old-moneyed bureaucrat. Not some beer-bellied, Busch Light–addicted, lazy-eyed drywall technician.

Anyway, I'm not sure why he goes by Bug, and I've never cared to ask.

Last time I saw him was during Christmas break, when I came home to find he'd turned my bedroom into his "computer room" where he could keep the "rig" my mom bought him. Funny how she couldn't help me out when my Honda needed new tires, but she could scrounge up enough nickels to buy him a $2,000 gaming system so he could play *League of Legends* all hours of the night with his smelly, overweight Doberman snoring at his feet.

I slept on the sofa for a few days, long enough to stick around for Christmas dinner with Grandma, then I hightailed it back to campus like my life depended on it. The sagging bed in my shithole studio was a million times more appealing than that nicotine-scented futon they use for a living room sofa.

"Should we cheers?" Lauren asks when our drinks arrive. I envy her blithe, light-as-air tone, the ease at which she smiles. She's always fucking smiling, like she doesn't have a concern in the world. And how could she? She's never known hunger or homelessness. She's never shopped at the Salvation Army or driven on bald tires for an entire winter. Lauren Wiedenfeld has everything a girl could ever dream of.

Of course she's happy.

As soon as Lauren lifts her martini glass with her perfect, manicured fingers, Tessa follows suit. Both of them glance toward me, waiting, *smiling*. I can't help but smile back at them, their happiness *almost* contagious. And I'd be lying if I refused to admit being treated like one of them, being included is a pleasant change of pace.

Lifting my glass, I meet theirs.

Three clinks.

Three sips.

Three . . . friends?

I've never had girlfriends before, but when I look at Lauren and Tessa, I kind of think it might not be so bad? That it might not hurt to try their world on for size?

Never know. I just might end up loving it.

3

Elisabeth Bristowe rests her hand on her belly before her palm circles it with the kind of tender gentleness only impending motherhood could impart.

"Tea?" she asks, as I wipe the marble counters in the recently refurbished kitchen of the nineteenth-century Victorian she shares with her husband. "I bought some Earl Grey . . . I know how much you love it."

Before I have a chance to decline—we're not supposed to accept gifts of any kind from clients—she's waddling toward the Keurig machine and dropping a pod inside. I'd mentioned, briefly, several weeks ago that I wasn't a fan of coffee, that Earl Grey was my hot drink of choice.

And she *remembered*. She didn't have to. But she did. And that speaks to the kind of person she is. Thoughtful. Compassionate. Detail oriented to a fault.

This woman doesn't miss a thing.

"Oh, did I tell you? It's a girl." Elisabeth hands me a navy-blue mug with a copper handle and some cheesy saying about coffee on the side. Her mouth pulls into the widest grin. She wanted a girl. She told me that once, in confidence. She wanted a little girl more than anything in the world.

I couldn't be happier for her.

"A girl? Congratulations!" I say. And I'm truly excited for them. Picturing Reed with a baby daughter wrapped in his strong arms warms me from the inside out. He's going to be an incredible father, the kind that will take her to the library on the weekends instead of planting her in front of an iPad. The kind that will take her on nature walks instead of dumping her at the childcare center of the local gym. And he'll read her books. God, will he read her books. Good ones. Time-tested ones. None of those cutesy anyone-can-be-a-children's-book-author kinds with the god-awful illustrations. "Any names picked out?"

Elisabeth takes a seat at the kitchen table, in front of the laptop that contains her newest work in progress. She's a novelist. The next hot thing, if you ask me. Women's fiction, mostly. Nothing fluffy or meaningless. Her books are the kind that gut you, that rip out your entrails before putting you back together. They have substance, staying with you for days, sometimes weeks, like a haunting melody playing on a loop in your head. They don't use cheap tricks or plot twists and they're not formulaic, mindless entertainment meant for the masses.

I would know.

She has me critique them for her from time to time, and she actually takes my feedback into consideration. She even changed the ending of her last book simply because I told her I wasn't feeling it.

"We have a shortlist," she says. "Reed wants to name her after his grandmother, Adelaide. I'd like something a little less old-fashioned."

I don't tell her that I think Adelaide is an adorable name. And that I can picture her already. Reed's dark hair and deep dimples. Elisabeth's hazel, almond-shaped eyes.

"What's at the top of your list?" I ask.

"I really like Mabry," she says. "It was my mother's maiden name."

Was. My heart breaks for a second. A year ago, I'd come in to find Elisabeth standing over the sink, tears in her eyes. It was then that she told me about the death of her mother, Cindy, who'd raised her as a single mom, working two jobs just to put Elisabeth through school. In the end, Cindy died sick and penniless, her death both a burden and a relief on her daughter, who'd been her primary caregiver those last years.

Elisabeth was racked with guilt and brokenhearted, but there was the tiniest hint of hope in her eyes. It was as if she could finally move forward, finally remember her mother as she once was and not as a frail bag of bones who couldn't remember her own name.

"Mabry Adelaide would be cute," I say, spraying the far side of the kitchen island with all-natural cleaner, though now that I think of it, I've probably already done this section.

It's easy to get distracted around Elisabeth. She talks to me like I'm a friend—and I suppose we are, in a way, though she's not the kind of person I'd call up when I'm bored. Maybe that's the true marker of genuine friendship? Either way, most clients aren't home when I come to clean, and if they are, they pretend I'm invisible—which is fine with me. But not Elisabeth.

Then again, she's a novelist who works from home and spends all day in front of a computer. I'm sure she's starved for human interaction and I happen to be convenient.

But I don't want to think like that. I respect her. A lot. And I like what we have—whatever it is.

I want to keep it that way.

"I suppose we'll have to compromise," Elisabeth says with a wink. "Anyway, we've got four months to go yet. Plenty of time to narrow it down."

The gentle scuff of footsteps in the foyer sends a quick jerk to my heart. I didn't know we weren't alone. A moment later, Reed appears in the kitchen doorway, attention directed toward his glowing wife. Without wasting a beat, he goes to her, bending to kiss the top of her head.

"You're going to be late," she tells him, lifting her hand to cradle his strong jaw.

"And it's all your fault," he says.

They share a knowing chuckle, and I imagine them tangled in their red flannel bedsheets this morning, their bodies melded, and it makes me blush.

The Bristowes are everything I hope to have someday and proof that not all married people are selfish assholes who don't take their vows seriously. These two are clearly in it for the long haul, and that's a fact that puts my cynical heart at ease every time I see them together.

"Meadow," he says, turning to me and straightening his tie. I love the way he says my name—enunciated, with intention. Like I mean something. "How's your morning?"

"G-great," I say. God, I hate when I stammer, but that intense, steel-blue gaze of his makes it hard for me to think straight sometimes. Clearing my throat, I add, "I heard you're taking over for Cutler's World Lit class."

His expression dissipates. Maybe I should've offered my condolences to Cutler's tragic situation first.

"So sad," I add quickly. "He's one of my favorite professors. I hope he recovers quickly."

Professor Bristowe's mouth forms a straight line and his hands rest on his hips. "Right, well, so far his prognosis doesn't sound hopeful. They're already talking about long-term care."

My hand covers my chest. "I'm so sorry to hear that."

"You're in World Lit, I take it?" he asks.

"I am." I crumple the paper towel in my hand before tossing it in the trash.

Reed passes me, grabbing his signature leather messenger bag off the back of a kitchen chair before slinging it over his shoulder. His spicy cologne fills the kitchen, mingling with the lemon counter polish I've been spraying. "Then I'll see you on Wednesday."

He offers a tepid smile, which isn't like him, but maybe he feels he can't be his usual charming self after discussing the near-death of his close colleague. But it was kind of him to say my name, to treat me like a regular fixture in his life and not some nameless face he sees wandering around the English department.

"Lis," he says to his wife. She glances away from her laptop and up toward him. "I love you."

She blows him a kiss and waves her fingers. And the second he's gone, she exhales. "Sorry about that. He's been really shaken up lately with the whole Cutler thing, and he's worried about taking on another class when his load was already maxed. He missed our birthing class last week. I think he feels like he's failing at everything right now."

Reed Bristowe could never fail. He's too hard on himself.

"That's a lot for one person to deal with all at the same time," I say.

"Exactly what I told him. He needs to cut himself a break. Just seeing him all stressed out makes me stressed out." Elisabeth adjusts her screen before placing her hands above the keys. "Oh, hey. Think you might have time to read for me this weekend? If I sent it to you by Friday?"

I glance up from the sink I've been polishing for the last two minutes. Every time one of Elisabeth's books drops in my lap, it's like Christmas morning. At least, the kind of Christmas mornings you see in the movies. My version of them wasn't exactly textbook. The number of years my mother cared to put up a tree I can count on one hand.

"Absolutely," I say, forcing myself to remain calm so I don't accidentally fangirl all over her like Kathy Bates's character in *Misery*. "Looking forward to it."

Grabbing my cleaning caddy, I head to the next room and get busy with the feather duster. This house is full of antiques, having been in the Bristowe family for generations, and I pride myself on never having broken a single piece—unlike the girl before me. I take care of their things as if they were my own, and Elisabeth and Reed appreciate that. They've said so, many times.

But it's my pleasure.

They're good people.

And I would do *anything* for them. All they'd have to do is ask.

4

"What size are you?"

I glance up from my homework-covered bed to find Lauren standing in my doorway Tuesday night. I haven't seen her since Monday afternoon, when I was coming back from work and she was leaving for class. And while I heard her rustling around this morning, I stayed in my room, hiding out until I heard the gentle slam of the front door. I don't want to wear out my welcome. I don't want to be everywhere, all the time. I don't want to annoy her.

"What?" I ask, though I know what she said. Heard her loud and clear.

"I'm going through my closet," she says with a sigh as she leans against the doorframe. "I'm in a purging mood. Was going to see if you wanted anything before I threw it out."

"You don't consign?"

Lauren's nose wrinkles. "I don't have time. Besides, I heard they only give you, like, fifty cents per item. Hardly worth the gas it takes to drive over there. I'd rather give these to someone I know. So . . . what size are you?"

I lift a shoulder. I don't know what size I am. I've always worn whatever fits, and whether it's baggy or tight is usually secondary to whether or not I can afford it.

"Stand up," she says, making her way across the room. Her gaze scans the length of me. "I bet we're the same size."

No way. There's no way. She's lithe and leggy with a defined waist and pointy shoulders. I'm . . . shapeless. Straight hips. Gangly arms. Knobby knees. Shitty posture. I'm not blessed with the kind of physique that begs to be shown off in tight sweaters and ass-lifting jeans.

"Here. Come with." Lauren's hand wraps around my wrist and she pulls me into her room, which is scented like lavender sachets and expensive perfume, and she steers me into her walk-in closet.

To call this expansive would be an understatement. By her standards, I'm sure this closet is considered small—most closets in older houses are—but she's managed to make the most of the space she's been given.

Jeans hang from wooden hangers, lined up in a row along the bottom. She must have at least twenty pairs, if not more. Above them are shirts, mostly blouses, with neutral shades like white and cream and gray and black, all color coordinated. Next to those are the colorful tops. Breton stripes, cashmere sweaters, the works. A shoe rack sits along the bottom of the closet, all of her heels and wedges and pristine sneakers neatly organized. Scarves and jackets and bags fill the rest of the space. How she's managed to make her closet look like a boutique display is beyond me. All I know is I can't stop gawking as Lauren is pulling pants and shirts and sweaters, all of it for me.

A minute later we return to my room, her with an overflowing armful of clothes, which she promptly deposits on my bed—burying my homework.

"Here," she says. "Try these."

She shoves a blouse at me first, her gaze fixated on the next item she's about to pull from the pile. I take the top from her, not like I have a choice, and wait. Lauren drapes a pair of jeans over her shoulder before turning toward me. Apparently tonight she's playing the role of my personal stylist.

"Try it on," she says, waving her hand because I'm taking too long.

"Now?"

She laughs. "Don't be shy."

My face heats. This is taking me back to seventh-grade gym class and the first time I had to change in front of other girls. I can still remember them standing in front of a mirror, comparing their nonexistent boobs and pinching each other's nonexistent belly fat.

With my back toward Lauren, I tug my T-shirt over my head and replace it with her blouse in record time.

Oh, my God.

It fits.

"Let me see," she says, words rushed and impatient.

I tug at the hem, adjusting the top, and then I spin to face her.

"Ohhhh, yeah." Lauren nods, handing off a pair of skintight jeans next. They're tiny, and there's no way in hell I'm going to be able to squeeze my ass into them. "Okay, you need to try these now."

"Maybe you could just leave them here?" I ask. "I really need to finish my paper. When I'm done, I'll try everything on and keep the pieces that fit?"

Her expression fades. Clearly she was in a mood to play dress-up tonight and I've ruined that for her.

"I'm sorry," I say. "I'm really behind or else I'd—"

Lifting a palm, she silences me. "Has anyone ever told you, you look like J Law?"

"Who?"

"Jennifer Lawrence. The actress." Lauren steps closer, her hand reaching toward my face as she tucks a strand of hair behind my left ear. I don't believe her. If I looked like some Hollywood actress my life would be a million times easier. She's just being kind. "Yes. I see it. Oh, my God. You could be her twin. You just need some highlights and maybe chop off about five inches of your hair. Side part. Loose waves. Perfection."

She makes it sound easy. Like *poof* and I'm pretty.

I can't remember the last time I had a haircut—at least one I didn't perform myself after watching a five-minute tutorial on YouTube. And I've never had highlights in my life. They seem like too much upkeep and way too expensive.

"I'm going to make you an appointment with my hair guy." Her mouth draws up at the sides. She's scheming, and I don't know how I feel about this.

"You don't have to do this," I say, hoping I can refuse her offer without having to bring my tight budget into this.

"Don't be ridiculous," she says. "If you're freshening up your wardrobe, you should at least freshen up the rest of your look."

"No, really. It's . . . it's okay," I say. Doesn't help that she's being so generous with her clothes. Makes it that much harder to offer her a firm no.

"My treat." Her manicured brows lift and her hands plead. "Meadow, I don't think you realize how gorgeous you are. It would make me ridiculously happy to help you see that. You're doing a disservice to yourself, hiding from the world. You should be out there, living your life, getting numbers, and breaking hearts."

I don't believe her.

But God, do I sort of want to.

Glancing at the pile of beautiful clothes resting on my bed, I think about all those times I convinced myself I was content to do my own thing, to never fit in. Conforming has never appealed to me. But the idea of strutting around campus in $200 jeans and designer sweaters with a cute little haircut could be fun? Maybe?

Not to mention these clothes are a million times better than the ones I currently have. They don't smell like a thrift shop. They're not holey or faded.

"Fine," I say. "You can make me over."

Lauren wraps her arms around my shoulders. We're the same height, the two of us, and she smells like sweet almonds and vanilla and the blossom of new friendship. All of it clings to me. To my skin. To my new shirt.

When she pulls away, she holds my gaze. "You're going to love your new look. I promise."

The instant she's gone, I lock the door and rifle through the items on my bed. Five pairs of jeans. Eleven tops. Four pairs of shoes—all of which are in perfectly fine condition if not a hair too tight, but I can make them work.

Stepping into the next pair of jeans and slipping the next top over my head, I stop and gape at my reflection in the dresser mirror. I don't recognize myself, at least not from the neck down, and I can't stop staring. Angling my body, I check out my ass. These jeans were cut to flatter and lift and nowhere do they sag or bunch. Even the length is perfect.

Unreal.

Over the course of a half hour, I try on everything—some things more than once just for fun—and when I'm done, I collapse on the heap of clothing covering my bed. Arms folded across my chest, I stare at the ceiling and just breathe.

This is a lot to take in.

In many ways, it's like I've won the lottery.

The lottery of clothing. Of friendships. Of roommates.

For the first time in my life, the gods are smiling down on me, giving me all the things I never knew I wanted.

Sliding my phone off my nightstand, I do a quick search for Jennifer Lawrence. I've heard of the name before and I know she was in those *Hunger Games* movies, but I refused to watch them out of principle. I didn't want to follow the crowd. Same with *Twilight*. *Fifty Shades of Grey*. But I digress.

I hit the motherlode with Google Images, and I click on the third image in the top row. Pinching my fingers, I zoom in, examining her typical white girl features. And then I see it. Full, youthful face. High cheekbones. Sandy hair. Hooded sapphire eyes. Maybe Lauren wasn't blowing smoke. We kind of do look like twins. But only if I squint hard.

Crazy.

Curious still, I go back to the results and look for the shoulder-length hairstyle Lauren was raving about, and I come upon an image of Jennifer, hair painted in shimmery blonde highlights, parted deep on one side, strands tucked behind one ear.

I could try this.

It's not like she's suggesting I chop off my hair and dye it blue.

Setting my phone aside, I gather the clothes and hang them neatly in my closet and try to put some order to them, the way Lauren did. When I'm finished, I stop to admire them.

A wicked smirk claims my lips when I imagine going back to my hometown, running into a local coffee shop where all the bitches from high school hang out during the summer, the ones who ditched college to marry their high school sweethearts and pop out their first babies before they were old enough to buy liquor. In my mind, I'm strutting past them with my trendy haircut and the kind of jeans that turn heads, brands that the girls in small-town Winterset have never so much as heard of because they're too stuck in their own bubble to open a fashion magazine or drive farther than an hour to go shopping.

They won't recognize me, and they sure as hell won't know what to think.

And I'll pretend like I don't even see them because they're beneath me. We'll come full circle.

Shaking my head, I rattle that silly little daydream away. Getting caught up in petty revenge fantasies when I have a ten-page paper due next week probably isn't the brightest idea. Flipping my textbook open, I try to focus on the paragraphs that fill the pages, but it's as if my mind doesn't comprehend them no matter how many times I read the same line.

All I can think about is me—the *new* me.

5

Lauren's phone keeps going off as we walk to World Lit Wednesday afternoon, matching almond milk green tea lattes (add two Splendas and a splash of sugar-free caramel syrup) in hand. I'm dressed in one of her outfits, sipping a disgusting beverage I only ordered because she wouldn't stop insisting, and listening to her prattle on about a guy by the name of Thayer Montgomery.

Her *boyfriend*.

I didn't know she had a boyfriend until a half hour ago, which says a lot about her. She isn't one of those women who define their self-worth based on whether or not they have a significant other. And she isn't one of those attached-at-the-hip-do-everything-together types either.

My respect for her has inched up another notch.

The tea tastes like a bunch of things that don't belong together, but I refuse to let five dollars go to waste so I try to distract myself by focusing on her minirant. A moment ago when we were in line, he was blowing up her phone while she was trying to order. Instead of silencing it, she shoved it toward me, rattled off her passcode (771562), and told me to text him and tell him she'd call him later.

"He's possessive and he doesn't even see it," she says, free hand slashing the air as she talks. "I can't even look at another guy without him getting all worked up. He's afraid he's going to lose me, but if he keeps acting like this, he *is* going to lose me."

"How long have you been together?"

Lauren glances up at the gray February sky. Her perfume is crisp and light in the cool air, wrapping around the two of us. I need to get perfume.

"Little over a year," she says.

"And has he always been this way?" I ask.

She exhales, her breath like clouds. "Always. That's why I told him we need a break. I can't take it anymore. I can't take the constant jealousy."

"Sounds insecure," I say.

Lauren is quiet for a second, and my heart trips in my chest when I worry I've offended her.

"He's extremely insecure," she finally responds. "And he has no reason to be. He's gorgeous and intelligent and he's *perfect*. Just wish he could see that."

We arrive at Patterson Hall and file inside, finding two seats side-by-side in the front row of the auditorium, directly in front of the podium. Lauren sips her tea, her matte magenta lipstick miraculously staying in place, and scans the room.

A few students pass, one of them giving me a double take, like I'm familiar but they can't place me. Or maybe . . . maybe they think I'm really something to look at? In a good way?

I don't want to get my hopes up.

Earlier today, I stopped at Target and splurged on new makeup. Thirty-two dollars later, I was the proud new owner of things like contour cream, dark circle corrector, liquid blush, extreme lengthening mascara, and 16-hour lipstick.

Thank God for YouTube tutorials or I'd probably resemble Ronald McDonald right now.

"There he is," Lauren says under her breath as she leans close. A waft of her expensive shampoo passes between us and she taps her taupe nails on my knee.

"Who?"

"Bristowe." She nudges me and I catch the Cheshire cat grin plastering her pretty face from the corner of my eye. "God, he's beautiful, isn't he?"

"Yep," I say. "And married."

To an equally beautiful woman. A woman who is very near and dear to me. An intelligent, talented writer. A thoughtful human being. The kind of person Lauren could never compete with.

Lauren shrugs, like it doesn't matter to her that he's a married man. My grip tightens around my pen and my breath quickens, but before I have a chance to say anything more, the lights flicker, Bristowe's signal for the class to be quiet.

I like Lauren, but this is just disrespectful.

I don't like the way she's looking at him.

Not at all.

6

Wellman's is packed Friday evening. Dollar wells tend to draw college students like flies to shit, which I think is a fair comparison. It isn't even five o'clock and half of these people are drunk off their asses on cheap beer, knocking into each other as they make their way around the room, screaming along word-for-word to the Imagine Dragons song blaring from the speakers.

It's pure chaos.

My shoes stick to the floor when I walk.

And I'm trying not to panic.

Instead I'm convincing myself that this is going to be fun, that I fit in more now than ever before. Lauren's guy cut and colored my hair today, Tessa picked out my outfit, and Lauren let me borrow a pair of sexy kitten heels that pinch my toes but add a boost of confidence to my walk.

We find an abandoned booth and steal it before anyone comes back to claim it. Squished between Lauren and Thayer and Tessa and a few other girls whose names I've yet to learn, I'm taking it all in. My hands are wrapped around a frosty beer stein and I'm choking it down, despite the fact that it tastes like bitter vomit and reminds me of one of my mom's exes who wore his perpetual beer breath like a medal of honor.

"Meadow, you want another?" Thayer asks, pointing to my drink an hour later. I've barely made a dent, but the beer is room temperature now, becoming harder to choke down by the second.

Tessa lifts a martini glass to her mouth, some kind of fruity concoction that's blue on top, orange on the bottom, rimmed in sugar, and garnished with a cherry.

"What are you drinking?" I ask her.

"A blue raspberry sunrise," she says. It's the dumbest name I've ever heard and exactly the kind of thing a new-moneyed college student would drink. "Want to try it?"

I point at her drink and yell across the table to Thayer. "I'll take one of those."

Anything would be better than lukewarm beer at this point.

Yanking a wrinkled ten-dollar bill from my wallet—a tip from yesterday's last client of the day—I hand it over. It kills me—kills me—to spend this kind of money partaking in an activity that makes me want to claw my eyes out, but if I'm forced to finish this warm beer, I'm going to be sick, I'm sure of it.

Thayer leaves, squeezing through the shoulder-to-shoulder crowd until he reaches the bar. Every so often, he glances back at Lauren, watching her. Or maybe watching to make sure she isn't talking to any other guys. Since the moment we arrived, she's been devoting her full attention to him. For someone who complains about his possessiveness, she caters to him like an exhausted mother to a petulant child.

I suppose she just wants to have fun tonight.

But Thayer seems polite, at least. He opened the car door for me when he picked us up an hour and a half ago. And he let me pick the radio station in the car, complimenting my taste when I went with the eighties underground channel.

When Thayer returns with my drink, I push my tepid beer aside and welcome the saccharin blue concoction with open arms. There's sugar on the rim. So. Much. Sugar. And there's no way this color of blue is found in nature, but I'm going to try to focus on the positives tonight.

These girls invited me here for a good time. They've slipped me a VIP, all-access pass into their world. And I'm not going to piss it away.

I'm going to embrace it. I'm going to plaster a smile on my face and force myself to be social even if it physically pains me.

It's the least I can do after all the nice things Lauren's done for me this week.

"It's our song!" Tessa squeals a moment later, her hand reaching across the table toward Lauren's. "We *have* to dance!"

The two of them shimmy out of our booth, not a care in the world. Within seconds, their arms are in the air, their hair bouncing on their shoulders, and they're laughing and dancing and living completely in the moment. They aren't concerned about how much money is in their checking account. Where their next meal is coming from. They aren't concerned about how they're going to pay rent or how the hell they're going to pay back a mountain of student loans after graduation.

Lauren and Tessa are 100 percent free.

And I want that. At least, as much of that as I can realistically have.

I don't want to care anymore.

I don't want to care about a damn thing.

Taking a generous gulp of my blue raspberry sunrise, and then another and another, I wait for the liquor to course my veins and bring me to where they are. That state of unadulterated freedom.

By the time the song ends and the two of them return, their faces flushed and glowing, my body is blanketed in warmth.

That was fast.

Then again, I shouldn't be surprised. My tolerance is extremely low, given the fact that I never drink.

"Meadow, you doing okay?" Lauren asks. "You're so quiet."

I hate being called quiet, even if I am. It suggests there's something wrong with me. And there isn't. Not everyone feels the need to hear the sound of their own voice twenty-four seven.

"I'm fine," I yell. It's perfectly okay to keep your opinions to yourself, to sit back and observe.

Everyone's eyes are on me, and everything seems to move in slow motion and everything sounds far away. It's almost as if my cares are slipping away in real time, drifting off one by one.

I need another drink, but the thought of squeezing through a hundred pushy drunks makes my stomach twist. All I can picture is getting shoved and trampled and ignored at the bar because I'm used to being invisible.

Tossing back the rest of my drink, I glance at Thayer, hoping he'll pick up what I'm putting down. Only he's completely fixated on Lauren, his stare intense and greedy, like she's the prettiest thing in the room and she can only be his. He hasn't stopped touching her all night, every chance he gets. His hands are constantly around her shoulder or cupping her face or he's interlacing his fingers through hers.

Possessive or not, she's lucky to have someone who adores her the way he does. Someone who would do anything for her. Who values her, who never wants to let her go.

"Eli's here," Lauren yells above the music.

Tessa follows Lauren's gaze, then reaches for her drink. She slams the rest of it back before excusing herself from the table for a trip to the ladies' room. The other girls follow, yet another typical girl behavior thing I've yet to understand. Who the hell wants an audience when they're doing something so private? I couldn't piss in front of another person if I tried.

A guy in a gray polo with wavy blond hair slides into Tessa's spot, his arm practically pressed against mine as his spicy cologne invades the tight space.

"Eli. What's up?" Thayer gives him some kind of handshake-high-five thing from across the table. I don't know what the hell it is.

"Thayer." Eli turns toward me next, eyes lingering on mine as a half smirk forms. "And you are?"

"This is Meadow," Lauren says. "My new roomie."

I hate that word. Roomie. But she's trying to be cute and it must work because everyone chuckles. These people are so damn happy, all of the time.

My hands begin to shake as Eli drinks me in, and I'm not sure whether I'm supposed to be formal and say, "Pleased to meet you" or if I'm supposed to play it off like I don't care about social graces, so I reach for my drink and bring it to my lips.

Only it's empty.

And now I look like a moron with zero social finesse.

"Whoops." Eli laughs at me. My ears heat. I fucking *hate* this. "I'm going to grab a beer. What were you drinking, Meadow?"

There is a God.

"Blue raspberry sunrise," I say, reaching for my purse.

Eli shakes his head. "I've got it."

Lauren and Thayer exchange looks the second he leaves.

"He's the cheapest son of a bitch I know," Thayer says. "And he's buying you a drink."

I shrug, like it doesn't mean anything to me. And it doesn't.

"He likes you," Lauren says.

"He just met me." I shake my head, hoping the dark lighting disguises the massive flush of my cheeks. "He doesn't like me."

"Fine, then he's interested," Thayer adds.

No guy has ever been interested in me. He's probably just being nice since I'm new to their little group. Or maybe he sees me as fresh meat, sniffing out my insecurities like a trained bloodhound.

He's a hungry shark and I'm chum.

Only unfortunately for him, I won't be had like that.

Tessa and her posse return and she slides into the seat Eli occupied just a second ago. A fresh coat of gloss makes her lips shine, and her hair seems to have been tamed back into place after that three-minute dance party a little bit ago.

She must like Eli.

And if that's the case—even if he *is* interested in me—I'm not touching that with a ten-foot pole. I like Tessa. And she likes me, I think. I want to keep it that way.

Just say no to girl drama.

My suspicions are confirmed the moment Eli returns and slides my drink across the table.

Tessa reaches for it. "Aw, Eli, you didn't have to—"

"That's for Meadow," he says, cutting her off. His eyes find mine, gauging my reaction. I bet he's the kind who likes to pit friend against friend. Sick bastard.

Her expression drops. She's confused. Or maybe embarrassed.

Shit.

"He was going to the bar, so I had him grab me a drink," I say. That explanation seems to satisfy her for the time being, but I can't help noticing the look she's shooting Lauren from across the table.

Is she . . . mad at me? Like it's my fault?

Lauren pouts, eyes sympathetic, then she glares at Eli.

I'm so confused.

A second ago, Lauren was pointing out Eli's purported interest in me . . . apparently knowing how her best friend felt about him. Now she's wordlessly communicating with Tessa about how much of a prick he is. Or that's what I'm gathering. I'm not yet skilled in the art of telepathic communication.

I've never understood the intricacies of female friendships, but this confirms everything I've ever assumed.

We're either allies or traitors.

Sometimes both at the same time.

And I can say this, since I'm a woman, but we are *not* to be trusted.

7

I'm stirred awake by the smell of bacon and eggs and a relentless throbbing in my head. Images of last night play in my mind, though most of it feels like a blur, like it all happened in a vacuum. The scariest part? I have no recollection of leaving Wellman's. I have no idea if we walked home, took the Tiger Jitney, or if Thayer dropped us off.

Everything after Wellman's is just . . . gone.

I don't like this feeling. I don't like that my memories were robbed, that they're erased forever. But I have no one to blame but myself.

Jerking the covers off my body, I place my aching feet on the floor and realize I'm in last night's jeans and top. Passing the dresser mirror, I catch a glimpse of a girl suffering her first hangover: mascara-rimmed eyes, smudged lips, crazy hair.

The fact that people do this again and again blows my mind.

There's nothing fun about the way I feel right now, nothing that makes me want to count down the days until we can do this again.

A burp forces its way up my throat, leaving the taste of stale, sweet alcohol on my tongue, which sends a churn to my stomach. I dash to the bathroom and brush my teeth twice before gargling with mouthwash until the inside of my cheeks burn.

When I'm finished, I head to the kitchen because I've never been this hungry in my life.

"Morning, sunshine," Lauren says, showered and dressed for the day, hair done and smelling like a rose—literally. Her back is toward me as she plates her breakfast and a carton of organic, free-range eggs rests on the counter, along with turkey bacon and fresh-squeezed orange juice. Her phone, which is docked on a speaker in the corner, plays some NPR podcast about climate change in the Northern Hemisphere.

It's a far cry from all those Saturdays waking up to the smell of Mom's greasy, post-sex breakfasts. I can't count how many times I'd stumbled into the kitchen to find her prancing around to Van Morrison in a tattered, see-through robe as her boyfriend-of-the-month waited for his meal at the head of the table.

I head to the cupboards Lauren designated as mine and retrieve a box of store-brand imitation Cheerios and a plastic bowl with a crack on the rim.

"How are you feeling?" she asks, taking a seat at the table. Her plate rests on a woven rattan place mat, her silverware on a cloth napkin. I wonder if being this formal all the time ever gets exhausting or if it's simply second nature at this point. And then I wonder if she's ever known what it's like to shovel cold cereal into her mouth while sitting in a living room watching *Green Acres* and *I Love Lucy* reruns on broadcast television because she doesn't have cable or satellite.

Doubtful.

"Just a little headache," I lie. More like a massive fucking freight train plowing through the center of my brain. I overdid it last night and I don't feel like looking like the novice that I am.

"There's aspirin in the cupboard by the sink," she tells me. "Help yourself. Help yourself to anything you need, always."

"Thank you." I pour my store-brand milk and grab a thin metal spoon from my drawer and take a seat across from her. "How did we get home last night?"

Lauren glances up from her plate. "You don't remember?"

I blink. Twice. Obviously I don't remember or I wouldn't be asking. "Everything's a little fuzzy still."

"You were talking to this guy," she says. "And then you left with him. Heard you stumble in around three AM."

Jesus. Who just lets their friend go home with a stranger? What if I'd been sexually assaulted or killed last night?

"I did?" I drop my spoon into my tasteless cereal.

"You two were all over each other, making out, getting handsy." Lauren laughs, stabbing her eggs with her fork. "We told you to get a room. Guess you took it literally."

I don't believe her.

I haven't made out with anyone since high school, and it was the geeky foreign exchange student from Holland who couldn't kiss worth shit and whose breath tasted like fish and Wrigley's gum—the kind in the white package.

But what reason would she have to lie?

I try not to act like it bothered me that my safety wasn't a concern of hers or that I'm questioning her interpretation of events. I'll know now for next time to contain myself a little more. Scary how easy it was for me to get caught up in the moment last night.

A couple of strong drinks and I'd left my insecurities and awkwardness at the door, embracing the attention guys were giving me, the free drinks that kept coming my way, the ridiculous selfies Tessa kept wanting us to take together. In fact, my face still hurts from laughing so much.

On some ordinary Friday night in February, I was one of them.

But for the life of me, I can't remember kissing or leaving with anyone. It's going to bother me all day, I can tell already. But this isn't the craziest part. The most insane thing about last night was that I enjoyed myself.

"Eli tried to get your number from me," she says. "You kept refusing to give it to him, so I told him no."

Thank God.

"Tessa likes him, doesn't she?" I ask. Pretty sure it's safe to say we're all friends now. I can inquire about these things.

She exhales through her nose, chewing her bacon and gazing out the window toward the snow-covered backyard. "It's complicated."

"I just . . . I noticed the way she kept looking at him," I say. "And she ran off to freshen up as soon as she saw him, like she wanted to look her best."

"It's a long story, Meadow." Lauren exhales, resting her chin on her hand as she holds my curious stare. I don't like the way she says my name, but I try not to take it personally. "Maybe she'll tell you sometime?"

We linger in silence for a minute too long before she rises and strides to the sink to wash her dishes. I've lived here six full days now, and I've yet to witness so much as a single dirty dish resting in the sink.

She's good at cleaning up after herself, making messes disappear.

"Anyway, I'm heading out." She yawns, stretching her arms over her head. "I'll be at Thayer's today. Probably stay there tonight, too."

"Have fun." I give a wave, a cutesy one with wiggly fingers like I've seen Lauren do with Tessa.

I could use a little alone time, a day to let my hair down and not feel like I have to be in full makeup and dressed to impress. This new me has been an exciting change of pace this past week, but I'm exhausted and I need a break. I need a second to just be . . . me.

As soon as I finish breakfast, I head back to my room and strip out of last night's wrinkled clothes, grab my robe and my phone, and head to the shower. While waiting for the water to heat, I decide to flip through my photos from last night in hopes they might jog my memory.

But they're all pictures of me with Tessa and Lauren, arms around each other, drinks sloshing in our hands, lipsticks matching.

No mystery man.

Tapping on my locator app, the one that tracks the whereabouts of my phone at all times should I lose it, I pull in a deep breath and prepare myself for a moment of truth. If I left Wellman's and went anywhere else last night, this will tell me.

Only everything is blank until three AM this morning when it says I arrived here at 47 Magpie Drive.

Someone cleared out my phone last night before taking me home.

8

It hits me as I'm knocking on Elisabeth's front door Monday morning that I completely spaced off her manuscript.

Shit, shit, shit.

"Meadow, good morning." Elisabeth answers the door, eyes lit and steaming cup of coffee in her hand. She's always so happy to see me. "Your Earl Grey is on the counter."

I need to tell her.

My mind races, searching for the right words to say, but everything circles back to the truth: I got caught up with some new friends and completely abandoned all responsibilities and prior obligations this weekend because I was too busy having fun.

Lugging my cleaning caddy and Oreck vacuum down the hall, my heart ricochets. I don't want to disappoint her, not when she's always so sweet to me. Not when I'm her number one fan. I'd hate for her to stop asking me to read for her. In fact, I'd be heartbroken.

"Okay, before you start cleaning. I'm dying to know . . . what'd you think of *The Mourning Glories*?" Elisabeth takes a seat at the head of the kitchen table, hands wrapped around her mug and all attention directed at me.

Drawing in a long breath, I gather my composure. "I'm so sorry. I meant to read it this weekend . . . I just—"

Her pleasant expression melts as she removes her gaze from mine. Pure disappointment. Exactly what I was afraid of.

"Oh. Um. Okay," she says.

I've never let her down before. Ever. I prided myself on being the one who would drop everything to read her book, who could fly through the pages, and give her valuable feedback even when pushing the tightest of deadlines.

I've skipped studying for tests, I've half-assed homework assignments, all so that I could prioritize her manuscripts.

"Elisabeth, I'm so sorry," I say, hands cupped against my racing heart. "I feel awful about it. I promise I can finish by tonight, though. Just give me until tomorrow to type up my notes?"

"No. It's okay." She waves her hand. "It's due to my editor tonight. I shouldn't have pushed it so close. It's my fault."

"No," I say. I hate that she blames herself. "I promised you I'd read it and I didn't. It's not your fault."

She rises, one hand steadied on the back of her chair and the other on her belly, and heads to the kitchen sink, peering out the window toward their extra-deep backyard filled with naked trees. Everything is so ugly this morning. The sky. The trees. The tension in the room.

"I'm so sorry," I apologize again, in case she didn't catch it the first time. I could apologize a hundred times and it still wouldn't be enough.

I should've read Saturday night, when I had the house to myself. Instead I played dress-up, like some superficial collegiate Barbie. I played with makeup looks and practiced top-knotting my hair. When I was finished, I lit one of Lauren's pricey boutique candles and put on one of her favorite downtempo music stations and paged through her newest issue of *Vogue*.

It was bizarre, I'll admit. Nothing I've ever done before.

But I was caught up.

Caught up in not being Meadow Cupples for a change.

"What's different about you?" Elisabeth asks a moment later. I didn't realize she'd been staring at me, and I'm suddenly wondering how long I'd been standing here, lost in space.

Reaching for my hair, I tuck a strand behind one ear before chewing the inside of my lower lip.

"Oh! You got your hair done. I like it," she says. It almost feels like things are shifting back, but there's still a melancholy tone in her voice. She's hurt. And I hurt her. "It's a good look on you."

"Thank you."

"What'd you do this weekend?" she asks, sipping her drink. It's funny, she cares more about the goings-on in my life than my own mother does. But at ten years my senior, Elisabeth is more like a surrogate big sister. "Anything fun?"

"I have this new roommate," I say. "She invited me out with her friends."

Her eyes squint, like she's piecing some kind of puzzle together. And I get it. New hair. New friends. New priorities. It all adds up. Elisabeth with her attention to detail figured me out in all of zero point eight seconds.

"It's good," she says. "To go out, I mean. To be social. When I was in school, all I cared about were books . . . and Reed. Kind of wish things had been different."

My brows meet. "What do you mean?"

"I never had any real friends. Never made any lasting friendships," she says. "Just wish that I had, is all."

There's a desolate tone in her voice, one that's probably been there all along. And it makes sense now. She works from home all day, has no friends besides her husband. She must be incredibly lonely now that I think about it. No wonder she chats my ear off any chance she gets.

The creak of the wooden staircase signals that for the second week in a row, we're not alone. Reaching for a bottle of countertop cleaner and a clean rag, I make myself busy. I don't want to gawk at the two of them again, and I have no business filling my mind with imaginings of their intimate moments.

Only there's no sweet goodbyes. No double talk. Just the jangle of keys and the stomping of leather loafers and the slamming of doors.

I glance up, only for a moment, and catch a look on Elisabeth's face—one I've never seen before.

And then I see the glassy sheen of tears forming in her hazel eyes.

She's pregnant.

Pregnant women are hormonal. They cry. And he's busy, the weight of the world on his shoulders.

There may be trouble in paradise, but like all storms, it'll pass.

I refuse to believe that it won't.

9

"I think someone was in my phone," I say to Lauren Monday night. We're both seated in the living room, noses buried in our homework. Up until tonight, I hadn't seen her since Saturday. Ever since getting back together, she and Thayer had been glued to each other's sides.

"Wait, what?" She glances up from the pale gray laptop resting on her thighs. "What are you talking about?"

"The other night. When we went out," I give her context. "Some stuff was deleted off my phone."

Her expression relaxes. "Oh. Jeez. You scared me. You probably bumped some settings or something. You were pretty wasted."

I start to respond but then stop. I don't buy it. I don't think even in my drunkest of stupors, I'd specifically delete the location data on my phone.

"I can't even tell you how many times I've found my phone in the fridge after a night of drinking. Or my keys in my shower. Weird stuff that makes no sense." Her gaze returns to her screen and she begins clicking away at the keys. "Anyway, don't you have a passcode on your phone?"

I nod. That and my thumbprint, which could easily be used if I'm passed out drunk.

"Did you update your iOS recently? Sometimes when I do that, I lose stuff or my settings get changed," she says.

"Nope."

"Was it scandalous, what they deleted?" she asks. "Pictures? Texts? Emails?"

"Nope. It was . . ." I exhale. I don't want to seem dramatic or like I've seen too many episodes of *Dateline*. "It was nothing."

"Okay, so don't stress." She glances at me once more, smiling, before shoving an earbud in her ear and returning to her assignment. Yanking it out a second later, she shoves her laptop aside and searches for her phone. "Crap. It's seven thirty. I was supposed to call my mom an hour ago." Lifting her phone to her ear, she covers the mouthpiece for a second. "Hey, I'm going home tomorrow night to grab a few things. You want to come with me? It's a forty-five-minute drive. I'd love the company. Gets boring."

Yet another first.

Meeting someone's parents.

There's a swirl of nervous energy in my middle, but my ego is flattered that she likes me enough to introduce me to her family. If nothing, it solidifies the fact that we're becoming friends. Actual friends. You don't take someone home to meet your parents if you don't like them, if they mean nothing to you.

I mean something to her.

"Mom? Hey." Lauren rises from her spot before I have a chance to answer. "Didn't forget you . . . the night just got away from me . . . Yep, it's all going well."

Her voice trails as she shuffles down the hall and a moment later, she's in her room, door closed. Returning my attention to Elisabeth's book—which I'm choosing to read out of equal parts enjoyment and guilt at this point—it isn't more than fifteen minutes when Lauren emerges, all smiles.

"My parents are so excited to meet you," she says. "We'll leave around four, if that's okay?"

"Sure." I try to inject a bit of enthusiasm into my tone, but I'm sure my apprehension is broadcasting via the worry lines spreading across my forehead. What if they don't like me? What if they think I'm awkward, weird? What if they can sniff out the fact that I'm dirt poor and they don't want me hanging around their daughter because our kinds don't mix? "Did you tell them I live here?"

Lauren's crystal eyes widen. "No. They have no clue. I just told them you were a new friend."

"Got it."

Lowering herself into her chair, she grabs her computer and returns to her music and gets back to work. I try to think of the last time I talked to my mom for no reason other than to catch up, but I can't remember. My freshman year, I'd call her to say hello every once in a while, on nights when I was feeling homesick for some insane reason and wanted to hear a familiar voice and she was the only real option I had except for my grandma, who was never much for talking on the phone. My mom would never make more than five minutes for me, always telling me she was on her way out the door with her man or meeting some friends for drinks at the square.

I didn't call her at all my sophomore year, thinking maybe she'd wake up one morning missing me and start making the effort.

Never happened.

Life never goes to plan for people like me. Only people like Lauren. It's like they're a magnet for good fortune, dreaming up whatever it is they need out of life and not blinking twice the second it manifests.

In the past eight days, it's almost as if *my* life is becoming a magnet for good fortune. I've landed a quiet rental in a nice neighborhood that doesn't break the bank, I've inherited a killer wardrobe, and I've amazingly been accepted into a group of friends who, so far, don't seem like snotty bitches.

And on top of that? I'm *happy*.

I'm truly happy. And I don't know that I've ever been truly happy in my life until now.

Maybe that's how these things work. You rub elbows with the lucky ones and some of their magic dust rubs off on you?

Whatever it is, all I know is I don't ever want to go back to the way things used to be.

10

"Welcome to Brunswick Cliffs" is chiseled into a rock next to an iron gate. Lauren swipes her card at the entrance and the doors swing open, my first foray into a gated community.

I try not to gawk at the mansions. They're ostentatious, over the top. They scream wealth and whisper secrets. Rich people always have secrets. But goddamn is this place beautiful.

Even covered in a blanket of snow, I can tell the landscapes are manicured and equipped with circle drives and elaborate water fountains that have been winterized. Naked trees line the streets, and I can only imagine how lush and full they look in the summertime, providing the local residents with cool shade as they zoom past in their imported sports cars and gas-hungry SUVs.

Lauren's car rolls to a stop at the corner of Primrose and Beaumont. Even the street names here are pretentious and upscale, at least to someone who grew up at 1534 West Twenty-Eighth Street South.

"We're here," she says as she turns into the circle drive of a massive white house on the corner. A covered porch spans the entire front of it and yet another porch rests on top of that one. It's like one of those Southern manor houses, only modern and updated with a million lights strategically placed to give it that "wow" factor the moment the sun goes down.

Lauren parks behind a dark gray Aston Martin with plates that say DOC W. Her father must be some kind of doctor. Probably one that specializes in weird shit and charges an arm and a leg for a basic consultation.

Climbing out of her car, I make my way between her Lexus and her father's Aston Martin where she's waiting to slink her arm into mine and lead me inside. Before we make it halfway down the brick-paved front walk, her mother is already standing in the doorway, arms outstretched like she hasn't seen her daughter in ages.

Lauren releases her hold on me and runs toward her mom's open embrace. I'd give anything to know what that feels like—to be missed, longed for.

"Mom, this is Meadow," Lauren says. "She's my friend from World Lit."

"Meadow, it's so lovely to meet you." Her mother's voice is warm bread and sweet honey. "I'm Suzette. Come on in."

We follow Suzette into a sweeping, two-story foyer, and I promptly remove my shoes at the rug. Grand crystal chandeliers cast shadows on the pale gray walls that lead down a hallway to the back of the house.

Passing through the hall, I find rows upon rows of family portraits, watching the evolution of Lauren from a newborn baby to a high school graduate. The girl couldn't take a bad picture if she tried. Shiny flaxen hair. Sparkling blue eyes. Perfect smile. As far as I can tell, she never had an awkward braces-and-baby-fat phase.

No one ever said life was fair.

Suzette leads us to the kitchen, where three small boxes rest on the table, and she removes the lid of the first one. "I hope you have enough here."

Lauren reaches inside, retrieving a handful of photographs before turning toward me. "It's my grandmother's eightieth birthday next month. I'm putting together this video with music and pictures for her party. It's a surprise."

Suzette beams, admiring her daughter the way everyone who ever comes around Lauren tends to admire her. "We can't wait to see how it turns out."

"Full disclosure, Thayer's helping me," Lauren says, placing a palm out. I recall how Thayer said he was a graphic design major the other night. It surprised me. He didn't seem like the type content to sit behind a computer monitor for hours on end, but then again, maybe I was comparing him to *League of Legends*–addicted Bug. Night and day, those two. Astroturf and crabgrass. "I don't want to steal all the credit."

"Either way, we can't wait. Nonna's going to love it," Suzette says, striding toward the oven and checking on a chicken roasting under the broiler. "Hope you two are hungry."

We seat ourselves at the table in the dining room, where her father, whom I've learned is a pediatric neurosurgeon by the name of Dr. Jay Wiedenfeld, joins us. He's friendly with young eyes that crinkle at the sides, a thick head of dark gray hair, and a dimple in the middle of his chin.

Suzette serves us an overabundance of food—roasted chicken and root vegetables, truffle risotto, honey butter croissants, and French silk pie—all of it made from scratch. If this is her way of showing off her kitchen prowess, she's awfully humble about it, chuckling off my praise before transitioning the subject.

I eat like royalty and she and Jay treat me like their guest of honor, asking dozens of questions and gushing over every answer I give, as if the most fascinating things in the world are coming out of my mouth.

It's the strangest sensation—being treated like you're special. It's like someone wove a blanket out of everything that's right in the world and then wrapped it around you like a hug.

It's almost addictive.

And it explains so much. People with money don't care so much about being perceived as rich as they do about being perceived as special.

I get it now.

When we leave, I'm buzzing. My entire body is humming with an electric charge. Already I can't wait to come back here, to dip my toe in the Wiedenfeld waters all over again. Maybe one of these weekends I can stay the night? I'd die. I'd literally die. I want to know what it's like to spend a day with this family.

I bet it's magical.

I bet they play tennis and watch golf and have cocktail hour and tell country club jokes and share pictures from their latest trip to Cannes.

I bet nothing bad ever happens behind these doors, and if it does, their housekeeper is on standby with a broom and dustpan to sweep it up and toss it outside where it belongs.

Lauren starts her car before my seatbelt is fastened. And then she yawns. It's dark out now, the sky starless, and we've got a little under an hour until we get back to Monarch Falls.

We stayed way longer than we'd planned, but her parents are expert conversationalists and it's like they knew how to draw me out of my shell. Once they got me talking, I couldn't stop. That's never happened before. It's like we just clicked.

Lauren sat there in silence most of the night, checking her phone under the table, completely bored with our conversation. Maybe she and Thayer are fighting again? I don't know. Or maybe she was jealous that her parents were fawning all over me? Hard to tell. I'm still getting to know her, still trying to figure her out.

"Your parents are amazing," I tell her once we hit the interstate. I can't stop replaying the night in my head, trying to record it like a movie, embed it into my memory.

She smiles, lips tight and tired eyes blinking as she focuses on the road.

"They're perfect," I say. Reaching for her radio, I twist the volume knob until her favorite band—which I've recently learned is Hooverphonic—begins to play, in hopes that it'll bring her out of her funk. "They really are. You're so lucky."

My words are met with zero response at first, and then she exhales. "There's no such thing as perfect, Meadow."

"You know what I mean," I say.

"Sometimes," she says, voice soft, "when you look close enough, you can see the cracks. And I think people who seem perfect are the ones with the most flaws. They just do a better job at hiding them."

I've never heard Lauren go so deep before, and I'm stunned into reticence.

"What you didn't see tonight," she says, "is the bottle of Riesling my mother downed before we got there or that the second we left, my father made a beeline to his study where he'll play online poker until one in the morning."

I'm not sure what to say, though I appreciate her openness with me, her honesty. She didn't have to tell me those things, but I love that she trusts me.

We're friends.

Lauren Wiedenfeld is my *friend*.

It never gets old, reminding myself of this new fact.

"Anyway, tell me about your family." I detect a hint of embarrassment on her end, the tiniest quiver in her voice. "Tell me your family proves my theory wrong."

Exhaling, I rest my forehead against the cool glass of the passenger window. "Wish I could."

"Really?" She takes her eyes off the road for a split second, long enough to look at me. "You seem so . . . normal. Like the daughter of a schoolteacher and an accountant, the kind of girl who grew up with a normal house and normal friends and a dog and parents that didn't put an insane amount of pressure on you to be exactly who they wanted you to be."

"I'd trade childhoods with you in a heartbeat."

For a moment, I think about opening up to her. Every story, everything I've ever resented my mother for . . . it's all bubbling to the surface, begging to come out. To be shared. I've never told anyone anything, ever. I've kept it all inside. Buried. Hidden like some shameful secret that defined the darkest parts of me.

"Okay, so what's your family like?" Lauren asks.

Pulling in a deep breath and feeling my self-control teetering, I begin. "I grew up with a single mom named Misty, and we lived in a two-bedroom rental that backed up to train tracks . . ."

I start at the beginning—which for me is when my dad left just after Christmas in first grade.

And I don't stop.

For forty-five minutes, I ramble on. I tell her *everything*. I tell her about all of my mother's boyfriends, the forgotten birthdays, the ignored Christmases, the empty kitchen cabinets, the stale bread and expired milk, the parties my mother would throw on school nights, the mean girls at school . . .

I hold nothing back.

I leave nothing out.

By the time we get home, I've bared my soul and it's terrifying.

But I'm liberated.

For the first time, I have hope. I have friends. I have a life. There's no sense in dwelling in the misfortunes of my past. From here on, I'm only looking up. I'm shedding this awkward and uncomfortable skin—no matter how painful this metamorphosis may be—in favor of something better.

And I'm never looking back.

11

The smell of dog piss and cigarette smoke smacks me in the face Saturday afternoon the moment I step inside my mom's house. I haven't even been here three seconds and already I can't wait to get back to my new place with its spot-free floors, flower-scented air, fluffed pillows, and made beds.

Let me make it crystal clear—I don't want to be here and this isn't a friendly visit.

I'm here on a mission.

I need money—more money—and this part-time Sparkle Shine Cleaning Co. bullshit job isn't cutting it, not since my tastes have shifted.

And let's be real. I'm not some idiot buying Louis Vuitton and Chanel. More like shopping the clearance rack at Nordstrom. But still. I can't keep recycling the same five outfits for the next three months. And I need shoes that actually fit, shoes that don't pinch my toes and blister my heels.

Mom and Bug don't acknowledge me when I walk in, their glassy gazes fixed on the TV where they're watching some 1970-style Western, the kind where the actors look orange and the cowboys shoot at everything that moves. Mom never liked this shit before. It's all Bug. But that's Misty Cupples for you. Tofu. Always morphing into whatever she needs to be, absorbing the likes and interests of the man keeping her bed warm at night.

Standing in front of the TV, I cross my arms until I get their attention.

"Contrary to what you might think, you are *not* made out of glass, Meadow Rain," Mom says. She still hasn't met my hardened stare. "Move it. Go find something to do."

Ah, that old sentiment.

Go find something to do.

If I had a nickel for every time she said that to me growing up, I wouldn't be here right now preparing to scrounge through my old belongings in search of things to pawn.

"Just need to know where you put my stuff," I say, keeping it brief and keeping my eyes from roving all over this junk-cluttered excuse for a living room.

Bug's fat Doberman growls. He hushes her with the wave of his hand and she lies back down.

"You know," I continue, "since you converted my bedroom into your computer room."

Bug squints at me before standing up. His pants fall a little, and he yanks them into place before walking to me.

"Misty, you better tell your daughter to watch the way she speaks to me in my house," he says, looking straight into my eyes. At least I think. One of them tends to wander, and I can never tell what he's looking at half the time.

"Your house?" I scoff at him.

He yanks his pants again before hooking his thumbs through the belt loops. "Damn right it's my house. You haven't lived here in years. Isn't yours anymore."

I begin to say something, but I stop myself. I don't need to get into a pissing match with a guy named Bug over who gets the privilege of calling this shithole "home."

Instead, I rise above it. I handle it with grace and class. The way a Wiedenfeld would. The way someone who knows their value and their worth would.

Bug isn't worth my energy.

"Just tell me where my things are," I say, one hand falling to my hip as I release a pressured breath. "I just want to take my things and go."

"Basement," Mom says, craning her neck to see the TV. After a second, she sits up, reaches for her pack of green Marlboros, and lights a new cig. "Storage room."

I hate that when I leave here, I'm going to smell like them. Like secondhand smoke, dog piss, stale clothes, and a greasy kitchen that hasn't been properly cleaned in at least eight years.

"Everything's boxed up with your name on it," Mom says. "Help yourself."

Tromping downstairs to our unfinished basement, I'm smacked with another overpowering odor. Flicking on the light, I freeze when I see a landmine of old, dried-up dog shit.

Dog. Shit.

Piles upon piles.

Just . . . hanging out.

Who lives like this?

Our basement is long and narrow and the designated storage area is at the far end. Watching my step and holding my breath, I begin my arduous journey past the land of dog shit and the puddles of dog piss (which have reduced to stains on concrete), and wind up in the valley of stacked containers of random junk.

Most of the cardboard boxes have Bug's name written on them along with the words "KEEP OUT!" because apparently he's a twelve-year-old.

My lungs drown in filth and dankness, and I'm moving and restacking boxes like a fiend until I find mine, all of them shoved to the back. Crushed. Crumpled. And somehow wet.

The window above must have leaked the last time the snow melted and my things were the proud recipient of the water that seeped into the basement.

Exhaling and trying not to lose my shit—there's enough of that down here already, I yank the lid off the first box. It's nothing but paperback books. Boxcar Children. Fear Street. Baby-Sitters Club. Nothing you couldn't buy on Amazon for a penny.

Grabbing the next one, I find my jewelry case. When I was eleven, my great-grandmother died, and my grandma let me have all of her old costume jewelry. I was convinced that one day it would be worth something, that there might be a rare precious stone or something worth an absurd amount of money. I dump the jewelry into my bag and move on.

The next box contains CDs, most of them from the early 2000s. No one listens to CDs anymore.

Junk. All of it.

The fourth and final box, which rested beneath all the other boxes, is in the worst shape. Sliding it across the floor, I hear the tinkle of broken glass.

God. Damn. It.

Lifting the lid, I find the yellow Depression-era plate my grandfather gave me, along with two matching glass birds that once belonged to his grandmother.

I'd been keeping them for sentimental reasons, though I'm not sure why. My grandpa was an alcoholic douchebag who beat my mother and her mother on the regular and died of cirrhosis of the liver after canceling his life insurance policy out of spite.

I bet I could've milked several hundred out of those pieces. If not more.

But now I'll never know.

I'll never fucking know because of *Bug* and his stupid fucking "rig" in his stupid fucking "computer room."

My breathing picks up. I've gone nose-blind to the shit and piss, thank God. Examining my surroundings, standing in the midst of the chaos, I decide to leave it all for them to deal with. I don't want any of my things anymore. They can burn in a fire for all I care.

I'm moving forward.

I want nothing to do with this life. This house. These people.

Stepping over one of Bug's many "KEEP OUT!" boxes, I accidentally kick off the lid. I have every intention of leaving it just like that, but morbid curiosity makes me turn around to see what could possibly be so important that he keeps it in a musty cardboard box in a dingy basement with a haphazard warning.

Lowering to my knees, I reach inside and retrieve a wooden box. Cracking the lid, I find bags upon bags of coins. Some of them in protective sleeves. Some of them rolled. Some of them in little cardboard displays. At the bottom of the box is a bag of gold coins.

For the record, I've never stolen anything in my life.

I don't believe in thieving and lying and the kind of things that make it difficult to sleep at night.

But then I think about the glass birds and how he essentially stole from me by damaging my personal belongings. He owes me. He owes me money. This is money. Coins are money. And if these were so important to him, they wouldn't be sitting here unattended to.

Anyone with half a brain cell would keep them locked up, hidden away.

I bet someone gave them to him a long time ago and he forgot all about them. Or he's holding on to them until they're worth more, which could be decades from now. Misty will be long gone from his life by then.

Shoving the bags of coins in my purse, I almost lose it when I find two more boxes of coins. And a gun. A Glock of some sort. Small.

Holy shit.

Nothing is locked. Everything is right there, begging me to take it, like some DIY karma intervention.

This is the universe's way of saying, "Sorry about the glass birds. Enjoy these gold coins we put in your path."

I take them all.

I feel like a giant piece of shit.

But I take them all and I put everything back the way it was before leaving.

I even take the gun—but only so I can toss it in the lake when I get back. Dipshit hotheads like Bug have no business owning guns.

Heading upstairs, I pass through the kitchen where my mom is grabbing food out of the fridge, onions, ground beef. She's cooking dinner, but she doesn't ask me to stay. Not that I would.

"Find what you were looking for?" she asks, back toward me.

"Nope," I say.

She shrugs. She doesn't care. She stopped caring a lifetime ago.

Mom shuffles toward the sink, her slight limp worse today than it was last time I saw her. When I was eight, she was in an accident. Hit by a drunk driver. She shouldn't have been out on the roads at two AM anyway, but she was coming home from the bar and met another driver who was also coming home from another bar.

If I thought my father leaving us destroyed her spirit, the accident was the final nail in that coffin. Left with a giant scar across her left cheek, a broken nose that never fully healed, and a gimp in her walk, she turned toward men for reassurance that she was still pretty, like before.

And God, did she used to be pretty.

She turns toward me. "You look different, Meadow. What'd you do?"

I shrug. "Cut my hair."

Her eyes squeeze. "Nah. It's more than that. You did something else."

"I cut my hair," I say again, firmer. "Highlights, too."

She points a pair of kitchen shears at me. "That's it. Highlights. Only hussies and high-maintenance bitches get highlights."

Ever since her injuries, other women—or at least women who Mom considers prettier than she is—are all either hussies or high-maintenance bitches.

"It's just something different," I say, reaching for my hair and smoothing a palm along the side of my head. "Doesn't hurt to change things up sometimes."

"Your clothes," she says. "They actually fit you for once. Do I *know* you?"

Turning to the pack of ground beef, she slices through the plastic with her scissors and huffs, laughing like she thinks it's funny that I look the way I do.

I have to remind myself that she's just jealous.

I'm no longer her homely-looking daughter, the one who could never outshine her. I'm blossoming into a beautiful young woman, one learning how to hold her head high, one getting hit on by cute college boys at bars, one with friends and a *life*.

It makes sense now, why she never taught me to do my hair. Never reminded me to wash my face or brush my teeth. Never taught me how to find a bra that fits. Never *once* took me shopping.

Misty Cupples didn't want to be upstaged by her daughter.

"I'm going now," I say, striding across the small kitchen.

"Meadow," Mom calls after me.

But I ignore her, the way she's ignored me my whole life.

12

I'm rich!

Okay, not exactly.

Let's just say I'm $31,261.35 richer than I was a week ago. A little less if you subtract the gently used Audi I bought to replace my rusted Honda. And the money I'm about to drop at the Berkshire Commons Shopping Galleria with Lauren.

"What do you think of this?" I hold a bottle of Maison Margiela perfume to Lauren's nose. I need a signature scent. Hers changes constantly, rotating between rose and lavender and almond and vanilla. Tessa's is gardenia, never wavering. Now I need one. I don't even know what I like. I've never worn perfume. All I know is that everything smells amazing and some of it makes me sneeze.

The attendant working the perfume section hands me a little jar of coffee beans to "cleanse my nasal palate."

Fancy.

"Love!" Lauren says. "You should get it!"

I flip the bottle over to look at the price tag.

One hundred and twenty-five dollars plus tax.

Jesus.

Though I dropped almost ten grand on the Audi earlier this week and have purchased a few other "incidentals"—a laptop, a new iPhone, a bunch of music Lauren recommended, groceries from Whole Foods—I still have a mini freak-out every time I spend more than five or ten bucks on something.

Being poor all my life, you'd think I'd have the good sense to hoard some of this. And I plan to. I'll put some of it away. But for now, I'm on top of the world, and I'm not quite ready to let that go.

"I'll take this one," I say, holding the bottle up to the associate. I tug on the hem of my top that rides up when I place the tester bottle back. It's a gray T-shirt sewn from the softest cotton I've ever laid hands on and it cost me an outrageous seventy-eight dollars at Anthropologie a few days ago. The phrase "la vie est belle" is scrawled across the front—which is fitting and symbolic.

La vie est belle. *Life is beautiful.*

Yes. Yes, it is.

The associate—whose name tag reads *Claudette*—smiles and points me to a register where she begins to wrap my purchase in glittery peach tissue paper and places it in a pretty little bag with baby-blue satin handles.

"Can we look at shoes next?" I ask.

"What kind of question is that?" Lauren nudges me. "Duh."

I'm going to need at least five pairs. Sneakers for trekking across campus, but cute ones. Flats—black and camel. Business professional heels for future job interviews. And something sexy and frivolous for going out.

Linking her arm in mine, Lauren guides me to the shoe section of her favorite department store and hooks me up with her favorite salesman, Todd, who treats me like royalty, complimenting my hair, laughing at everything I say, ignoring all the other customers in favor of devoting his full attention to *moi*.

And that's what this is about. It isn't about the shoes or the money.

It's the star treatment.

It's the constant endorphin high.

The dopamine rush.

I am adored.

Maybe I'm selling out, maybe the old me from several weeks ago would have a conniption if she saw me now.

Or maybe not.

Perhaps she'd pat me on the back and say, "Well done, Meadow. You're finally getting *exactly* what you deserve."

13

47 Magpie Drive is lit from within Tuesday night. The house is buzzing with music—Tessa's pick . . . Zero 7. Candles are burning, infusing the air with magic. On the stove, the teakettle whistles and outside the wind howls.

Every few minutes, this flood of warmth washes over me. My heart flutters. I catch myself smiling for no reason.

This is home.

It may be temporary, but I belong here. I live here. I sleep here every night.

These are my friends.

I have friends.

Lauren Wiedenfeld and Tessa Barrett.

It's only been a few weeks now—enveloping myself in this new way of life—but it's crazy how easy it's been. Some nights, I lie in bed, staring at the ceiling, wondering how I got this lucky. Wondering why fate decided to place me in Lauren's path the way it did. And right before I finally drift off, I pinch myself. A reminder that this is real. That I didn't dream this into existence.

Tessa flops onto Lauren's bed, settling herself among the fluffy white pillows and thumbing through her phone.

"Who are you stalking?" Lauren asks. I think she's kidding, though.

"Eli." Tessa exhales, slamming the phone face down. "I need someone else to stalk."

Lauren's seated at her desk chair finishing off an email when she swivels in my direction. "Anyone you want to stalk? Tessa is amazing. She can find out anything about anyone. Just give her a name and she'll give you their entire life story in less than ten minutes. I'm serious."

I smirk, glancing down at my recently manicured hands. I had my first gel manicure this week. It was forty dollars plus a tip, but the girls both said they swear by these and the nail technician promised they'd last three weeks. Lauren picked the color—taupe.

"Actually," I say. "This guy in my art history class asked me what I was doing this weekend."

Lauren's jaw falls. Tessa's, too.

"Wait, what? When were you going to say something? What's his name? What did you tell him?" Tessa sits up.

They're glued to me. This is major news and their eyes dazzle, like they're happy for me, like they're living vicariously through me.

"His name is Brent Miller," I say. My chest flutters when I think about the way he looked at me today. Completely captivated. The feeling was mutual.

Tessa is already on her phone and Lauren scoots her chair closer.

"What'd you tell him? Did you say yes?" Lauren asks.

"Holy shit. He's fucking hot." Tessa flashes her screen in our direction. It's his student ID photo, which she promptly found on the Tiger Paw Portal. "He's a graphic design major. Wonder if Thayer knows him? And he's a junior. From Eden Prairie, Minnesota. Living in the Keystone Campus Apartments. Here's his number."

I bite my lip. "He already gave me his number."

Lauren jumps in her seat. "Call him! Call him right now."

Their nervous energy is mingling with mine. I'm sure if I called him right now I'd be a bumbling, stuttering, stammering mess. I couldn't possibly be smooth with these two staring at me with wide eyes and gaping mouths.

"Guys, you're making way too big of a deal out of this," I say, half chuckling. "I told him I'd think about it. He gave me his number. I don't want to seem desperate."

"Good point." Tessa directs her attention my way before looking at Lauren. "She's right. She should play hard to get. Make him work for her."

Lauren releases a contemplative breath, sinking back into her rolling chair. "Yeah. Agree. Call him next week."

I've never had a boyfriend, much less gone on a date, but I won't tell them that.

"I'm so excited for you, Meadow," Lauren adds. "Maybe we could double date or something?"

"We should," I say, maybe a little too enthusiastically. But the idea of a double date and having some of that pressure taken off me sounds amazing. I'm still new at this stuff.

"Awesome. I'll text Thayer." Lauren grabs her phone and the room is silent.

"I'm starving," Tessa says a minute later, climbing off the bed.

"It's eight o'clock at night," I say. "And it's minus three degrees outside."

"Me too. I forgot to eat today." Lauren laughs, standing and blowing out one of the candles on her desk. The room feels darker, like someone sucked all the life out of it.

And who just . . . forgets to eat?

"You want to get something with us?" Tessa asks, hands sliding into her back pockets as she looks me in the eyes. "I'm thinking sushi."

Tessa knows I don't like sushi.

14

The girls left fifteen minutes ago, and according to Lauren's Insta account, she's already tagged herself at Taki and posted a selfie of the two of them cheersing with their fourteen-dollar Japanese martinis.

I can't help but feel slighted here.

Left out—intentionally.

And I get that Lauren can be oblivious 99 percent of the time, but Tessa isn't. She's astute. And she knew exactly what she was doing.

My skin is on fire and I'm pacing the house, my mind racing. Weeks ago this sort of thing wouldn't have bothered me. Weeks ago I wouldn't have even cared about being included. Weeks ago I'd have shrugged it off and locked myself in my room.

Granted, I could have gone. I could have ordered a Sunday roll and a seaweed salad and a god-awful drink and cheersed along with them, but my gut told me Tessa didn't want me there.

Oh, my God. She's jealous.

She's jealous of my friendship with Lauren. I'm a threat to her. That's all this is.

Fucking girls and their fucking drama.

I thought better of Tessa, too.

Stomping to my bathroom, I tie my hair into a messy bun on top of my head—Lauren taught me—and wash the makeup off my face, patting it dry with a fluffy hand towel. When I glance up at myself, my skin is ruddy, my eyes squinty. I look like the old Meadow.

Lonely. Bitter.

The girl who had a bone to pick with life.

Dragging in five long, deep breaths, I straighten my posture and reach for my toothbrush, reminding myself it's okay to spend an evening alone. That FOMO—fear of missing out—is a stupid term coined by millennials who are too insecure to admit they enjoy their own company from time to time.

I do enjoy my own company. Always have.

But I keep seeing Tessa's stony gaze, feeling the coldness in her words.

And it hurts.

Snapping myself out of it again, or at least attempting to, I groan when I realize I'm out of toothpaste. I'd meant to run to the store earlier after class, but I came home to Tessa and Lauren and the night evolved into an impromptu hang out session.

It's way too fucking cold to leave the house now.

With my toothbrush in hand, I tiptoe down the hall toward Lauren's room. I'll just use her toothpaste. If she were here, she wouldn't mind. And I'd do the same for her.

Her door swings open with a quiet creak, and I step inside. It feels wrong being in here, without her, but I trudge ahead, flicking on the light and making my way to her bathroom.

It still smells like the perfume she sprayed on twenty minutes ago, moments before they loaded up their coats and scarves and boots and braved the cold for the love of fucking *sushi*.

The bottle, pale pink and cut crystal, rests on the vanity, unlidded. I lift it to my nose and inhale the sweet scent. Before I realize what I'm doing, I spray it onto my left wrist. The bathroom already smells like it and she won't notice. It'll be faded by the time she returns anyway.

The perfume warms on my skin, making the top notes richer and the middle notes more vibrant—I learned all about "notes" from Claudette at the department store. It's Versace. I commit that to memory. Maybe I'll buy that next? A girl should have more than one perfume, I think. A scent for every mood.

The left drawer of her vanity is sticking out, and I catch a glimpse of her extensive makeup collection. Clear bins fit together like some sort of puzzle, each one containing similar products—one for mascaras, one for foundations, one for eyeshadows, one for tweezers and clippers. Her right drawer contains skin products. Vitamin C serums. Eye creams. Acne gels.

I don't spot a single drugstore brand.

Lauren's bathroom is basically a mini Sephora and everything is calling to me. The pretty packaging. The gorgeous palettes. The delicate mink makeup brushes.

Reaching for a peach palette covered in gold lettering, I click it open and find a set of six cream blushes. Two of the six are mostly used up, the other four untouched.

Swiping one of Lauren's favorites—a pale pink—onto the pad of my middle finger, I dab it onto my cheek. But it doesn't look right. I need foundation.

We're completely different skin tones—she has pink undertones and I'm more olive skinned, at least that's what the lady at the department store said to us one day. But I want to try some of these, I want to compare them to my own, see if they're worth the extra thirty or forty bucks an ounce.

Selecting a bottle of Dior foundation, I apply it all over my face with my fingers before carefully rinsing my hands in her sink, using enough soap so that when I dry them, there won't be so much as a trace of foundation on her pink hand towel.

Next, I return to the blush bin, only I try a different color. This one is a powder, which I apply with a bushy brush that feels like a million bucks on my skin.

By the time I'm finished, I'm not sure how long I've been standing here, but the girl looking back at me in the mirror has a full face of designer makeup on and she's smiling.

I like this Meadow better than the ruddy-faced, pissed-off version.

This Meadow has doors opened for her, guys that pick up the pens she drops in classes. This Meadow gets compliments on her shoes from other girls. This Meadow has learned to stop blushing when she feels the lingering stare of the opposite sex. This Meadow raised her hand in class the other day, made a joke—which the entire class found hilarious—and then found herself stopped in the hallway afterward by a tall drink of water named Brent Miller, who asked if she was new.

And she said yes. Yes, she was new.

Because it was true.

The way I carry myself has completely changed, and it's only drawing good things into my life. I could never go back.

Never.

And fuck Tessa for feeling threatened by me.

She *should* feel threatened by me.

15

I've seen a lot of shit in my day.

But this?

This?

No. I refuse. I refuse to believe this.

This changes *everything*.

I wait behind a vending machine on the fourth floor of the English building because Lauren is headed this way. Lauren. My roommate. Whom I just spotted leaving Dr. Bristowe's office with tousled hair and red lips suggesting an intense make-out session—or something. She was giggling. He was leaning in his doorway, one arm up as he glanced down at her. One of his shirttails was untucked—a massive red flag as his normal state of dress is nothing short of impeccable.

She twirled her hair.

And smiled.

He kept his voice low.

And smiled.

This wasn't a professional interaction.

This wasn't a faculty member mentoring a senior on her capstone project.

They did something.

My stomach rolls and I hold my breath, listening for the soft tromp of Lauren's sneakers as she heads for the elevator.

She passes, not noticing me in my fur-trimmed parka—the one exactly like hers but black instead of green.

Sweet, oblivious Lauren.

We're supposed to go out tonight. Wellman's. Lauren, Thayer, Tessa, me, and some of the others.

I'm not sure how I can do that now. After what I've seen. The way they were looking at each other is going to be burned into my memory for the foreseeable future. Already I must have replayed their little interaction a half a dozen times.

Doesn't she know his wife is *pregnant*?!

Does destroying someone's family mean *nothing* to her?!

I see red. And then nothing. When I come to, I find myself slumped on the floor and good old Margaret Blume is asking if I'm all right. She doesn't recognize me. Then again, she hasn't seen me in a month. I probably wouldn't recognize me either.

Rising, I brush my hair out of my face, suck in a deep breath, and nod before dashing toward the stairs. I won't take the elevator. I don't even want to touch anything Lauren has touched in the last five minutes. Maybe that's petty, to feel that way, but I'm disgusted.

I want nothing to do with her.

If only it were that easy.

16

I said I had a migraine.

It's a perfectly infallible excuse. No one can deny that I have one. They can't see it. Can't test for it.

The moment I got home this afternoon, I barricaded myself in my room and locked the door. When I heard Lauren's voice an hour later, I slipped my earbuds in and played my music. Bowie, Queen, Lynryd Skynrd. None of this Esthero, Tosca bullshit.

When she texted me about going to Wellman's, I told her I had a migraine. She replied with some emojis. A sad face. And a blue heart. Ten minutes later she texted that she hoped I felt better, that they'd miss me, and that she was going to Tessa's to get ready.

She also asked if I needed anything. Chicken soup. Hot tea.

This isn't a fucking sinus infection.

I didn't reply.

Maybe I should have. But technically someone with a migraine wouldn't be on their phone. The lights are too bright or something.

Turning my music down, I wait for her to leave, listening for the gentle slam of the front door and the soft purr of her Lexus engine. A minute later, I watch her back out of the driveway, texting on her phone and nearly hitting our mailbox.

Funny how before I didn't mind her texting on her phone. Now it annoys me. I think it makes her look careless, selfish.

As does sleeping with a married man.

Granted, I don't know if they're having sex, but a dashing thirtysomething professor and a pretty little student like Lauren wouldn't be risking their academic careers for blow jobs and titty fucks.

And furthermore, she's a liar. A dirty, dirty liar.

And I fucking hate liars.

Even if she's lying by omission, it's still lying.

It's insulting, offensive.

Did my friendship mean nothing to her?

She could ramble on and on about the details of her menstrual cycle and the particulars of her and Thayer's robust sex life, but she couldn't share this?

Does Tessa know? Does Thayer? Is that why he's so possessive of her? Because he knows he can't trust her? Does everyone else know except for me?

I stop pacing the apartment, but only for a moment. Glancing at my hands, I notice I've chewed my nails to the quick, my gel manicure demolished.

Fitting.

My stomach growls, but I couldn't eat if I tried. It would all come up, I'm sure. Instead, I fix myself some hot tea, only the second I reach for one of Lauren's mint jade-green tea sachets, I stop myself.

I need to separate myself from her. I need to unadopt all the things that have made me into a knockoff version of the very kind of person I never wanted to be.

Dumping the hot water in the sink and the tea sachet in the trash, I pour myself a glass of tap water—lead levels be damned—and march straight to her room.

I don't know what I'm looking for, but I'll know it when I see it.

Shoving her bedroom door so hard the knob hits the wall, the coiled doorstop springs, and the stupid thing nearly ricochets back into my face, I step into a cloud of Lauren's Versace perfume.

It makes me gag.

I'd open a window if it weren't five degrees out.

Her room is immaculate. Bed made. Pillows fluffed. Clothes neatly hung in her closet. Her collection of perfumes resting in an aesthetically pleasing order on the clear acrylic tray on her bathroom vanity. Her makeup drawer is intact, still organized to a T.

One of her many spare purses—the Louis that she uses the most—hangs off the back of her desk chair. She must have taken her Chanel clutch tonight, the black leather one with the silver chain strap. Bet she's wearing her black kitten heels, too. The ones with the red bottoms. I check her closet to confirm, finding an empty spot in her shoe organizer where those heels are typically perched.

I laugh when I think about how well I know her. And then I laugh again when I think about how I truly don't know her at all.

Taking a seat in her swivel chair, I rest my elbows on the desk and hold my head in my hands, breathing in, breathing out. I don't know what I'm doing in here. I don't know what I expected to find other than a bunch of pretty things.

This makes me feel dirty. And it's all Lauren's fault.

I wouldn't be doing this if it weren't for her deceit, her double life, her phony half-truth friendship that I no longer wish to have.

Lifting the lid of her laptop, I type in the six-digit passcode to her phone on a whim, not expecting it to work.

A soft jingle plays and her screen comes to life.

Holy shit.

Everything is neatly organized into folders coded with her class names: *ENG423*, *ENG370*, *PSY334*, *ENG430*, and *MA393*. I double-click all of them, examining every document, every subfolder, looking for clues or codes or hidden files intentionally mislabeled.

I find nothing.

It takes me an hour, maybe longer, but I go through everything. Except her email. It's password protected and probably contains an entire collection of Lauren Wiedenfeld's secrets. Exhaling hard, I adjust my posture and try to crack it. I try Thayer's name, Bristowe's name, her passcode backward. I try her middle name (Aubrey). I try our address.

I try her birthdate. I try endless combinations of every "Lauren" thing I can come up with.

I try and try and try until I'm finally locked out.

Rising from her stupid chair (that she casually mentioned cost a pretty $1,200), I accidentally knock over her stupid Louis bag (that she casually mentioned cost a pretty $2,200).

Bending to retrieve it and trying to remember exactly how it was draped over the chair back, I grab the lip balms and hand creams and perfume minis that fell out and freeze when I catch the glint of a familiar necklace.

A tarnished silver chain holds a silver-plated heart, the initials *MRC* engraved on the back.

My initials.

This necklace was a gift from my mother on my fifth birthday—the last birthday we ever celebrated, when my dad was still there and he wheeled out a pink bike with yellow training wheels and a giant purple ribbon attached to the handlebars.

He got me a bike. Mom got me a necklace.

I outgrew the bike but I kept the silver-plated heart, holding it as proof that once upon a time we were a happy, normal family.

It makes no sense why Lauren would steal this. The chain is chintzy and delicate, the heart discolored. This thing is hardly wearable and even if it were, it wouldn't be anything that would coordinate with Lauren's cashmere sweaters and designer jeans.

As much as it pains me, I slip the necklace back into her purse. If I take it back, she'll know I was in here, going through her things. And I don't want her to know that I'm onto her, that I'm going to find out exactly who she is.

And when I'm done?

She'll wish she never met me.

17

Lauren didn't come home this morning. She texted me saying she stayed at Thayer's after Wellman's last night and that she was planning to stay there all weekend. She then told me to text her and let her know if I needed anything.

I need the truth, Lauren. That's what I need.

Once again, I didn't respond. I sat at the kitchen table eating a cold bowl of fake Cheerios without a place mat (*gasp*), and I stared out the window toward the backyard with its patches of muddy, melted snow and ugly, naked trees.

I don't know how I ever thought this was picturesque.

It looks like a toxic wasteland. Everything is dead.

Last night brought me three, maybe four hours of sleep. The rest of the time I tossed and turned, wrapping my head around all these theories and probabilities, trying to explain what the hell Lauren wanted with my necklace.

The Bristowe thing? That's something else. The necklace has nothing to do with that, as far as I can surmise.

Sometime around three AM, I sprung out of bed and took inventory of my belongings. I thought maybe . . . just maybe . . . she was a klepto who got off on stealing. Kind of like Winona Ryder in the early 2000s.

But a half hour later, everything was accounted for.

Dumping my cereal bowl and shuffling to the shower, I make myself presentable and decide lunch with Tessa should be on the docket for the day. Not because I want to, but because I have to. She's Lauren's closest friend, and if I can ask the right kind of questions, I might be able to glean a little more insight into Lauren's character.

Perched on the edge of my bed an hour later, a towel wrapped around my wet hair, I suck up my pride and text her. Ever since that weird sushi night she's been distant with me. Used to be she'd text me memes and pictures of hot guys from campus when she'd be sitting around bored in her business admin classes.

But those all stopped the last few days. She went cold turkey on me. On our friendship.

My message consists of the word "lunch" and a question mark. I follow up with a sushi emoji.

I will shove raw fish down my throat until I puke if it means getting some answers.

Three gray dots bounce on the screen before disappearing. She read my message, began to respond, then deleted it. She must be thinking about how to get out of this, how to say no. Or maybe she's texting Lauren, asking if she wants to come.

God forbid Tessa does anything without Lauren.

I'm about to place my phone down when it vibrates in my hand.

Her message consists of the word "time" and a question mark.

We settle on one o'clock.

18

I order the spicy tuna roll and a saketini.

Tessa doesn't comment about me not liking raw fish and I don't comment on the fact that she ordered tempura chicken. I bet she only orders real sushi when Lauren's around. And I bet when you boil Tessa down to the bones, she's a small-town girl just like me who saw a bit of the girl she wanted to be in Lauren Wiedenfeld and somewhere along the line lost herself trying to become her.

We probably have more in common than Tessa realizes, but I'm not here to discuss that.

"Where's Lauren?" Tessa asks. Like she doesn't already know.

"She's staying at Thayer's all weekend." I sip my martini. It's disgusting. I smile. "This is so good. Want to try?"

Tessa sips from the clean side of my glass. "Amazing. I should get one next time."

"You should." I glance at her water glass. If Lauren were here, she'd be drinking.

For a Saturday, this place is dead, and our food arrives in record time. The tinkle of chopsticks on plates fills the booth we share, and I chase every bite of my tuna roll with a gulp of my martini. I'm going to be lit by the time this is over.

"Tessa," I eventually say. She looks up, chewing, her rosebud lips neat and tight and her round eyes trained on me. "I wanted to ask you something..."

This feels like an episode of *Real Housewives of Meyer State University*, where two of the women are about to have a confrontation about an incident that happened earlier. All we need is a camera crew and a producer with a headset and clipboard.

"What's up?" she asks, playing dumb. Girls do that. We play dumb. Especially when we sense impending conflict.

"Did I . . . did I do something this past week? Something that upset you?" I ask, forehead wrinkled and voice soft so as not to put her on the defense. I need this to go smoothly. I need her to feel comfortable opening up to me or she'll never tell me anything about Lauren.

"What are you talking about?" She seems legitimately confused. And I almost buy it.

"You just seem a little distant lately," I say, glancing down at my plate like I'm sad. "Maybe I'm imagining it."

Tessa laughs, reaching across the table to swat my hand. "Oh, my God. Meadow, you had me so nervous for a second."

I laugh, shadowing her body language. "So, I didn't do anything?"

"Of course not." She sits up straighter. "I had midterms and a paper to write and . . ."

She rattles on. One excuse after another. They seem convincing, but that isn't hard to do.

"I miss your memes," I say. We share a giggle. "Did you ever ask that guy out from your chem class?"

The air is lighter, the mood lifted.

This is what girls do.

We stab each other, we dress our wounds when we're done, and we ignore the scars that remain.

"I didn't ask him out," she says, as if her lack of courage is embarrassing. "Guess I'm still hung up on Eli." Tessa reaches for her water, silent for a few beats. "I just want what Lauren and Thayer have, you know?"

I lift my drink. "Amen."

"They're just perfect together."

"Aren't they?" I sip. "How long have they been together now?"

The longer I can keep her talking about them, the more likely she'll be to let something slip.

Her brows meet. "I have no idea. A year? Maybe more? You'll have to ask her."

"Can I ask you something?" I lean in closer. She follows suit. "Lauren always says he's possessive, but I think he seems nice. He doesn't . . . do anything to her, does he? I know sometimes people can act one way when they're around someone new and then act a certain way around other people. Didn't know if maybe he's always on his best behavior around me?"

Tessa's face hardens and then relaxes. "He likes her a lot. I think sometimes he can be intense, but she's a big girl. If he ever crossed a line, she'd kick him to the curb. Don't think for one second Lauren isn't in the driver's seat of that relationship."

"Okay." I smile, as if I'm relieved. "I just wanted to make sure he wasn't . . . doing anything to her. As a friend, you know? I worry sometimes."

"Of course. We all do." She takes a drink of water. Her tempura chicken is half gone. "I'd be the first to kick his ass if he pulled anything with her. I'd make my brothers drive all the way here from South Dakota, baseball bats in hand."

She chuckles, but I read between the lines. She's affirming her position as #1 friend. But lucky for her, I'm not bidding for that position. I just want answers.

"How did they meet? Lauren and Thayer?" I sense that we're running out of steam here. She's yet to so much as hint that there might be a load of dirty laundry between those two.

"Mickey's maybe?" She lifts a brow. "We met him one night when we went out. That's all I remember. We were probably doing a pub crawl. Yeah. Last St. Patrick's Day I think?" Tessa pushes her plate a few inches forward. She's already finished eating. Or maybe she's done with this conversation. "Why are you asking me so many questions about them? Why not just ask Lauren?"

Oh, my astute little South Dakotan princess.

The way she's looking at me, one eye half pinched, makes me think her assumptions are headed in the wrong direction. She probably thinks I *like* Thayer and that is *not* where I want this conversation to veer.

Shrugging, I place my chopsticks on my plate. "Just making conversation."

Tessa nods, arms folded across her lap as she chews her inner lip. "Okay, if I tell you something, do you swear not to repeat it?"

Now we're talking.

"Absolutely," I say. "I swear."

"Thayer . . ." She sucks in a deep breath. "I mean, he's never hurt her. He's never laid a hand on her." Wrinkling a napkin in her hands, she closes her eyes. "But . . ."

She's taking way too fucking long to get to the point.

"He has all of her passwords. He knows her schedule. Sometimes he'll drive by barre to make sure she's there," Tessa says. "Like I said, he's intense. But when it's good, it's really good. That's what Lauren says. And she seems happy, so I don't say much. But I mean it, if he ever hurt her . . ."

So, Thayer's a prick.

That's all the dirty laundry she has?

Talk about a waste of a forty-dollar lunch.

"Is there a reason you think Lauren stays with him? Besides it's 'good' sometimes?" I ask. This is like squeezing blood from a stone.

Tessa shakes her head. "No clue. She says she loves him. It's not for me to question."

Of course it isn't. Tessa's afraid if she speaks up, she'll lose Lauren's friendship.

"You two tell each other everything, right?" I ask. She nods. "Then you should tell her how you feel."

She smirks. "Lauren doesn't always like to hear the truth."

"What?" I pretend I didn't hear her in hopes she'll elaborate.

"Nobody likes to hear the truth when they're in love," she says. The phrasing changes, painting Lauren in a more flattering, generalized light. It's completely intentional. "Anyway, I'm meeting a study group in twenty minutes. Care if I bail?"

Shit.

I didn't want to end on this note—talking about Lauren. I wanted to veer away from this, have a bit of casual conversation, and end on something neutral.

If she saw through any of this, I'm fucked.

"Of course not," I say, watching her rise and fish around in her Louis until she hands over two crisp twenties.

Tessa slips her coat over her shoulders and fastens the toggle buttons before checking her phone. Her fingers tap the glass in record speed, and I worry she's texting Lauren about me and I hate that I care if only for a fraction of a second.

"Oh, real quick," I say before she turns to leave. This may be one of the last times I get Tessa alone, and I have to ask. "Do you know Emily Waterford?"

Her nose wrinkles. "Who?"

"Emily Waterford." I don't elaborate.

"Never heard of her." Tessa adjusts her bag over her shoulder. "Why do you ask?"

My lips part and I'm seconds from coming up with some kind of bullshit excuse, but I stop myself. If Emily lived with Lauren last year, Tessa would've met her at some point and she wouldn't be staring at me with this baffled look on her face.

"Forget it," I say, forcing a tight smile. "You should get going."

Something isn't adding up, and until I figure out why, I'm keeping my cards close to my chest.

19

Today marks the first time I've ever called in sick to Sparkle Shine Cleaning Co. It's Monday. And I couldn't bear to see Elisabeth, not after knowing what I know. Looking into her eyes and pretending like I don't know the fate of her future is something I couldn't bring myself to do, so at six AM, I called the shift supervisor and left a message saying I woke up with a terrible cold, hanging my head upside down off my bed so I sounded nasal.

I'm not proud.

I simply did what I had to do.

Dressed in shades of brown and cream, clean faced, and hair tucked beneath an army-green knit cap, I've been trudging around the snowy campus all day, following Lauren and keeping my distance.

I've followed her from English class to English class, watched her duck into the library between classes, and stop at the Hub to meet a friend for lunch. She checks her phone constantly, another little quirk of hers that used to not annoy me. Now I want to smack the stupid thing out of her manicured little hands.

Around three o'clock, she leaves her last class of the day, straightening her hat and trekking toward the bus stop.

Again, I stay back. Watching.

Only she gets on the blue bus instead of the green.

There are eleven stops on the green bus, all of them on the north route. Our stop is on the south route.

Bristowe's office—the English department's building—is off the blue route.

Maybe I'm a glutton for punishment, or maybe for once I want to prove myself wrong, but I head in that direction, looking like a maniac in my snow gear, running across campus. But at least I'm an invisible maniac. No one's checking me out today.

Slipping and sliding, my breath clouding the air around me, I manage to make it there in under ten minutes, just as Lauren is entering the main doors.

Holy shit. I was right.

I wait a few minutes before going in, and then I take the stairs to the fourth floor. Lauren never takes the stairs. Less of a risk of her seeing me.

When I arrive, I wait around the corner, taking cover behind the noisy Coca-Cola machine with a perfect view of Bristowe's office.

She shouldn't be here—not for school reasons. Her capstone meetings are on Fridays. This is a Monday. Lauren should be on the green bus, going home.

Their voices fill the quiet hallway, tones pleasant and laced with excitement. I peek around the vending machine in time to see him usher her in.

He closes the door softly before drawing the blinds to the window looking into the hall.

My eyes squeeze, burning then watering. I imagine him setting his picture of Elisabeth face down. I imagine her reaching for his belt, him slipping his fingers in her hair. Two wicked smiles. A shared secret.

It isn't right.

Lauren has no right to ruin Elisabeth's happiness.

Perhaps, then, it's only fair that I ruin hers?

20

Thayer gave me his number the night we first met. At the time, I thought he was just being polite . . . like an "any friend of Lauren's is a friend of mine" sort of thing. Now I know he wanted to create that connection in case he ever needed it or if ever he couldn't locate his beloved. As her roommate, I was a link to her. A way of tracking her down.

But I'm flipping the tables.

My phone trembles in my unsteady hands but I manage to tap out a coherent text. With a hovering thumb, I read it over and over again. Once I send this, it can't be undone. It'll be there, forever.

The message is simple, unassuming, but the intention is nothing short of nefarious.

DO YOU KNOW WHERE LAUREN IS?

Pacing, I draw in a cold breath that freezes my lungs and hit send.

Within seconds, it's delivered and subsequently read. Three bouncing dots fill the screen and then disappear.

My palms sweat. I've never done this before. Never interfered like this in anyone's relationship—not even my own mother's, and believe me I had ample opportunity to take some of those sons of bitches down.

The ring of my phone sends a shock down my spine despite the fact that I fully expected this.

He's calling.

"What are you talking about? I thought she was at home?" he asks before I get a chance to say "hello." His words are rushed, breathy. Sprinkled in anxiety. He doesn't like to be left in the lurch.

You and me both, Thayer.

"She's usually home by now," I say. "I texted her earlier but she didn't respond."

It's a dangerous lie to tell, especially when I could so easily be proven wrong, but I don't want to lose my momentum just yet. I'm so close I can taste it.

"Jesus." He's panicking. I'm imagining his palm dragging the length of his handsome face. His shoulders slumping. His breath growing heavy. "I haven't heard from her in hours now that I think about it."

"It's probably nothing. I just didn't know if she was with you."

"She texted me after class. Said she was on her way home."

So the bitch flat-out lied to her own boyfriend. At least I'm not the only one she's keeping secrets from.

I don't tell him I saw her take the blue bus and stop off at Bristowe's office. I'll let him piece this puzzle together himself.

"Let me call her," he says, working himself into a frenzied, frantic state.

I kind of feel bad for him now. He's nothing more than a pawn. But it's for the best. She doesn't deserve him. She doesn't deserve a man who adores her so much he worries about her when he hasn't heard from her in a couple of hours.

I may not be the most experienced woman in the relationship department, but I'm pretty sure that's love.

"If I don't hear from her, I'm coming over," he says.

I lift a brow. What good will it do if he comes over? It won't make her instantly appear.

"I want to be there when she comes home," he says, tone lower.

Oh. I get it. He wants to catch her in her lie. That's what this is about.

"Of course," I say, biting the shit-eating grin on my face. In my mind's eye, they're screaming at each other, embroiled in a lover's quarrel that can only end in one way. And I'll be locked in my room, listening from the other side and waiting until he says those three little words . . .

"We are done."

"See you in a bit, Thayer." I hang up and pray he gets here before she does.

This is going to be good.

21

For four hours, Lauren's been MIA.

She doesn't answer her cell, doesn't reply to text messages. If I didn't know precisely where she was, I might be concerned for her safety, but instead I'm sitting here, sipping a glass of cabernet (and pretending I like it), watching Thayer stand by the living room window, surveying the driveway for the glowing xenon headlights of Lauren's Lexus.

When he isn't staring out the window like a puppy waiting for their master to come home from work (or a jealous boyfriend waiting to catch his cheating girlfriend in a lie), he's pacing the house.

Also, he's on his third beer in an hour.

I figured it wouldn't hurt to add a little fuel to the fire by way of alcohol. I know from eyewitness experience that drunk fights are the most destructive . . . emotionally and otherwise.

"You should sit down," I tell him, reaching for the remote that controls Lauren's sound system. One of her favorite bands comes on and I tune it to another playlist immediately. One of mine. An eighties mix.

Thayer exhales and takes a seat in Lauren's chair, which makes me think he must not be that mad at her if he's willing to sit there. Then again, maybe he isn't petty like girls are. Maybe he doesn't overthink and overanalyze like we do. Maybe he wears his emotions on his sleeve and that's what gets him in trouble most of the time.

Lauren thinks he's possessive because he's insecure.

I think it's just because he loves her.

And why wouldn't he? She's practically perfect in every way . . . if you know nothing about her secret dealings.

"You like the Velvet Underground?" he asks, pointing to the speakers. "Turn this up."

Angry Thayer is now Distracted Thayer.

"I don't like the Velvet Underground," I say. "I love them."

He cracks a slow smile. His teeth are big and white but they fit his face perfectly, balancing his square jaw. Dragging his hand through his dark hair, he leans toward me.

"Thanks for letting me know about Lauren," he says. "It's nice she has someone who worries about her as much as I do."

I don't know if I'd put it that way . . .

"I probably worry about her too much." His tone is self-deprecating and he glances at his hands. How someone so low maintenance could wind up with someone as high maintenance as Lauren is beyond me.

Thayer pulls his phone from his pocket for the millionth time, checking his screen, darkening his screen, sliding it back in.

"Has this happened before?" I ask.

He glances up. "What?"

"Lauren disappearing," I say with a smile, rolling my eyes. "She's so oblivious most of the time. You know how she is. I just wonder if maybe she changed her plans and her phone died or something."

His brows meet. "Every once in a while, yeah."

"Oh. So this isn't the first time?"

His lips flatten. He doesn't respond.

"Do you think . . . do you think she's with someone else?" I plant the seed that's probably already there, but at this point, the more the merrier.

Germinate, little seeds.

Grow.

"I probably shouldn't say this." I keep my voice down and garner his full attention. "I mean, she's my friend and all. It just seems like you two are constantly fighting, and clearly you don't trust her."

Thayer's elbows dig into his knees and he buries his head in his hands, exhaling through his fingers.

Have I struck a chord? A nerve? Anything?

We share a silent moment, and I'm desperately hoping he's letting my words sink into the deepest parts of him. I barely know Thayer and yet I know one thing: he deserves better than her.

"Lauren is—" he begins to speak when the front door flings open and a gush of cool night air chills the living room.

Speak of the devil.

"Where have you been?" Thayer goes to her side without hesitation. And his tone is more worried than angry.

I don't understand.

"I thought you were coming home after class today," he says.

Lauren's gaze passes between us as she unwraps the Burberry scarf from around her neck. "What are you doing here?"

"You didn't answer your phone. We've been trying to reach you all afternoon," he says.

Shit. She knows damn well *I* didn't try to get a hold of her once.

"My ringer must be off." Lauren unzips her coat before placing it in the closet by the front door. "Were you worried about me or something?"

Thayer exhales, pinching the bridge of his nose. "I wouldn't have come here if I weren't."

She lifts a brow. I think she's still confused. Rising on her toes, she kisses him, playing it off like it's nothing and quashing any chance they had of fighting.

"You worry too much," she tells him, tapping her pointer finger against his broad chest. "It's cute, but let's dial it back, okay? Like we talked about before?"

He says nothing.

I've wasted my time.

It's going to take a lot more than this for him to see the light. He needs concrete evidence. Emails. Pictures.

Damn it. Why didn't I take a picture earlier?

"How was work?" Lauren asks, taking the spot next to me on the couch. I breathe her in, searching for a hint of Bristowe, but all she smells like is cold air.

"Fine," I lie. "How was class?"

She sinks back, drawing her knees to her chest. "Midterms. That's all I'm going to say."

Thayer is still quiet, though he's watching her. I can only hope the wheels in his head are still spinning, that he's smart enough to see through her sweet little shtick.

"I feel like I haven't seen you at all lately," she says. "I miss you."

She *misses* me?

"We should do lunch tomorrow. There's this new café downtown I've been wanting to try," Lauren says.

She's up to something.

"Sure," I say. If I say "no" in front of Thayer, after playing the part of the dutiful, concerned friend, it'll be a huge red flag.

"You sticking around?" she asks Thayer as she rises from her seat. "I'm just doing more studying tonight. Pretty boring."

He stands. "Yeah. For a little bit."

She slips her hand in his, leading him to her room. I bet it's the very same hand she used to grip Bristowe's cock just hours ago. No shame. No shame at all.

I wait for them to disappear before returning to my room, locking the door—on principle, not because I have to—and lying on my bed, hands clasped on my stomach and gaze stuck on the motionless ceiling fan.

Tonight was a massive failure, but I'm not deterred.

I'm just getting started.

22

There are a lot of things that have no business being together.

Lauren and Thayer and Lauren and Bristowe, for example.

And then there's the bizarre excuse for an entrée sitting before me. Fennel-roasted chicken. Jicama. Farro. Dried cranberry. What the fuck is this shit?

I pick out the weird bits and slice into my organic, grass-fed chicken breast. It's okay.

Lauren inhales her roasted kale and portobello salad like it's her last meal on earth, and she's already talking dessert. *Squash* pie with a graham cracker crust.

Hard pass.

I swear this place has a bunch of monkeys in the kitchen, throwing shit together and charging an arm and a leg for it. And idiots like Lauren eat it up because they're certain eating something besides steak or a burger or a plain old chicken sandwich makes them special.

"You're extra quiet today." Lauren laughs, stabbing her kale. "What're you thinking about?"

I shrug. "The future."

Her eyes widen and she nods. "It's scary, isn't it? Not knowing what comes after this . . . if everything's going to work out exactly the way we planned . . ."

"What do you see for yourself?" I ask, locking gazes with her. "You want to get married and have babies or do you want to do the millennial career-woman thing?"

"Can't a girl have it all?" She winks, taking another bite of salad.

I don't appreciate her dodging my questions, making light of them. "Do you want to get married, though? You and Thayer seem pretty serious."

Lauren almost chokes, knocking her fist against her chest. "I don't see myself marrying him, no. I kind of don't really believe in marriage. I think it's an antiquated concept, just like monogamy."

Now it's my turn to choke. I reach for my water to wash it down.

"I've yet to meet a single married person who hasn't grown bored after the newness wears off," she continues, obviously speaking about Bristowe.

I hate her even more than I did before, and I didn't know that was possible.

"Then why waste your time with Thayer if you have no intention of taking it to the next level?" I ask.

Her glossy red lips twist into a smirk. "Good in bed. Fun to go out with. Hot as hell. He's the trifecta of boyfriends."

Cat's got my tongue and I'm stuck inside my mind, hurling insults at her at warp speed. My fist clenches under the table, my nails digging into my palm.

"I'm just being honest," she says, perhaps sensing my disapproval. "We're friends. I'm supposed to be able to tell you these things. Woman to woman." I remain silent. "What, it's okay for guys to brag about using girls for sex, but we can't?"

Oh, Lauren.

It's not that. It's not that at all.

"At this point in our lives, we should look at men as disposable and temporary. We should be having fun." Lauren continues to try to justify her behavior.

"I guess it's all fun and games as long as you're not hurting anyone, right?" I ask, thinking solely of Elisabeth and her unborn child.

"Exactly!"

23

"Lauren here?" Thayer stands at our front door Thursday night, half past six.

Lifting a brow, I tell him, "No. She's at barre."

He pushes past me. "Drove by. She wasn't there."

Nice. I don't even have to play dumb this time. I had no idea she wasn't at barre.

"Have you tried to call her?" I ask the obvious.

"Several times. It goes straight to voicemail." He's pacing the living room now, releasing hard little breaths as he grips his knit cap in his hands.

"You want a beer?" I ask. I need him primed and ready for when she finally arrives. Maybe Monday's situation wasn't enough. He needed to see for himself that she was up to no good.

Thayer doesn't answer, he tromps to the kitchen and helps himself. The crack and hiss of his can is all I hear a moment later. Ooh, he's all kinds of worked up!

"Where do you think she could be?" I call to him.

"Who the fuck knows," he calls back. When he finally returns, he plops down in the center of Lauren's pristine sofa and kicks his snowy shoes up on her beautiful glass coffee table. So he does have a little spite in him. "I've been thinking, Meadow. About what you said the other day."

Yesssss.

"And you're right. I shouldn't be with someone I can't trust," he says, stretching his hands behind his head. His body is relaxed, surrendered, but his words are terse. He's all kinds of confused right now, one giant contradiction.

This is a man in the midst of making a *major* decision.

"What am I even doing, Meadow?" he asks.

I don't know how to answer him without showing my true colors. "What do you mean?"

"She's hot one minute, cold the next. It's been this constant up and down from day one," he says. "And it drives me insane. The colder she is, the more I want her. That's fucked up, isn't it?"

"No. That's reverse psychology." It never once struck me that maybe Lauren knew exactly what she was doing. Maybe everything is a game to her. Some people get a kick out of fucking with other people's emotions, having power over their psyches. "We always want what we can't have."

I'm leaning against the back of Lauren's favorite chair when our gazes catch. In a perfect world, I'd be good for him, I think. I wouldn't string him along or leave him hanging. I wouldn't tease him for worrying about me. I wouldn't hurt him the way Lauren does.

I'd be gentle with his heart. And I imagine he'd be gentle with mine.

We'd have it all, Thayer and me.

Life could be so perfect if only Lauren would disappear.

24

My gel-manicured fingers are wrapped around a martini glass at Wellman's Friday night. What appears to be a cosmopolitan is actually cranberry and water. No alcohol for me tonight. I've got work to do.

Across the table, Lauren and Thayer are making out. Hardcore.

Last night was another big fat failure. I don't know what it is with these two. Some people just like dysfunctional, fucked-up relationships. They're drawn to them like moths to flames. They can't resist.

My mother is the same way. I hate that Thayer is cut from the same cloth as her. Kind of ruins him for me.

Tessa's been unusually quiet all evening, though she's wasting no time tossing them back. Probably because Eli's here with someone else.

"Ignore him," I say, nudging her arm. "You're so much prettier than that girl anyway."

She reaches for her hair, but her eyes are trained on them. "You think?"

"Absolutely," I lie, taking a sip. The girl is gorgeous. In the unfair kind of way. Almost reminds me of a young Elizabeth Taylor, all black hair and curves and turning heads everywhere she goes.

"I'm going to run to the ladies' room. Come with." Tessa slips her Louis clutch beneath her arm and slides out of our booth. I follow because I've been waiting for this all night—a chance to get Tessa alone.

My attempts to destroy the fucked-up-ed-ness that is Thayer and Lauren have failed. I'm moving in on Tessa.

The bathroom smells like bleach, vomit, and sewer water, but it's miraculously clean. Tessa slicks her third coat of lipstick on her full lips before fussing with her hair. She hasn't said a word to me yet, and I'm not quite sure why she wanted me to accompany her. Guess Lauren was a little . . . preoccupied.

"What is it about Eli?" I ask, climbing onto the Formica counter, hands gripping the edge.

Her dark brows rise. "He's everything."

I try not to roll my eyes. When someone describes something as "everything" they're just being lazy. These laptops and iPhones are melting our brains, I swear. We can't even form coherent sentences half the time.

"What do you mean?" I ask.

"He's pre-law," she says, like that's supposed to impress me. "And he's going to Harvard for law school in the fall."

I find it hard to believe that some previously poor girl from Middle of Nowhere, South Dakota, wants to chase after some prick who's going to school to become an even bigger prick.

"Lawyers are assholes," I say. "You don't want that. You're way too nice."

She laughs through her nose. "He's nice, though."

"Really? He shows up here and hits on other girls right in front of you every Friday night. He brings girls around knowing you like him. That's not nice. That's called being a douche canoe," I say. "The first night he met me? Bought me a drink."

Her head cocks toward me. "You said you asked him to grab you one at the bar."

Rolling my eyes, I say, "I know what I said. But I didn't want to upset you. Lauren told me you liked him."

Her eyes soften, like she's realizing I might not be so bad after all. Ha.

"Anyway, I didn't want to tell you this," I begin. "But since we're talking about that night . . . Thayer and Lauren were kind of . . . I don't know how to put this . . . they kept telling me Eli was into me and they were kind of making a thing out of it."

Tessa drops her lipstick into her clutch. "What do you mean? Making a thing out of it?"

I shrug. "I don't know. Pointing it out? I just thought it was odd since they both knew how much you like Eli. Thought it was shitty of them, actually."

Her chin lowers and she huffs. "Yeah. That is shitty."

Mission accomplished. Seeds of friendship doubt are officially planted.

Hopping off the counter and washing my hands because I feel gross being in here for this long, I turn toward Tessa and offer my most sympathetic, "I hope I didn't make you feel bad."

She's quiet, and I'd give anything to read her thoughts.

"Just . . . please don't repeat it," I say, because that's what girls say when they tell secrets and betray one another. "I don't want to start a thing with you and Lauren. I just thought you should know. I'd want to know."

"I won't say anything." She messes with her hair for the tenth time, making it worse with each brush of her hand. Her posture deflates and she looks like she wants to be anywhere but here.

"Let's do a shot," I say. "On me. And then we'll dance. If I have to show the DJ a little nip so he'll play your favorite song, I will."

She cracks a half smile before linking her arm in mine. And I smile, too. Because I've got her exactly where I want her.

Tonight she's going to see that *I'm* the fun friend. *I'm* the good, true friend.

And she's never going to look at Lauren the same again.

I may not have been able to steal her boyfriend, but her closest friend is kind of the next best thing.

For now, I'll take it.

25

"Feeling better this week, Meadow?" Elisabeth Bristowe answers the door with a pale pink mug of steamy brown liquid and a twinkle in her eye. "Made you a tea."

I lug my caddy and vacuum into her foyer. "Thank you."

"I missed you last week. Was worried when they sent someone else," she says as we head to the kitchen. She places my drink on the island. "I swear, no one cleans this place the way you do. I don't know what I'd do without you."

"I graduate in May . . ." I say.

"Don't remind me." She takes a seat at the table, next to her closed laptop. A notebook lies beside it, open to a page scribbled with notes. She must be planning her next book. Rubbing her hand on her belly, I swear she's gotten bigger since two weeks ago. "Did I tell you Reed's aunt is throwing me a baby shower this weekend?"

I'd heard all about Reed's aunt before. In fact, I met her once. Sweet as sugar and cute as a button. She raised Reed from the time he was seven, Elisabeth told me. She couldn't have kids of her own or she never married—I don't quite remember—but she's basically his mother. I never did ask what happened to his parents. It doesn't seem like my place to pry.

"Sounds like fun," I say, squirting some marble polish on her countertop. "Excited?"

"You should come."

I freeze, wondering if I misheard her.

"I want you there," she says. "It would be nice if there were more people there than just family."

In other words, she doesn't have many friends. Which I always assumed, but this confirms it. And it's a shame. She's the sweetest. The kind of thoughtful soul anyone would be lucky to have in their life.

"It's at the community center," she says. "Saturday at noon. And you don't have to bring anything."

"Don't be ridiculous." I already know what I want to get her. I saw it at the mall a couple of weeks ago: a cashmere teddy bear and a silver rattle. Keepsakes. Things Baby Girl Bristowe can have forever. None of this disposable, destructible, grow-out-of-it-after-a-year shit.

Her Calacatta gold marble gleams under the sunlight that pours through the window above the sink. Spring is just around the bend and the warmer temps melting the snow is helping to turn the grass green. I even spot a few little buds on some of the maples in Elisabeth's backyard.

Sometimes we die a little so we can be reborn, stronger than we were before.

"We're naming her Mabry," Elisabeth says. "I got my way."

"As you should." It's the least he can do for her.

"I think I might look into getting a doula," she says. "You know, one of those support people that stay by your side during delivery. I mean, Reed will be there, but he's been so preoccupied with work lately, I'm worried he's not going to know what to do." Elisabeth chuckles. "He's missed three birthing classes now. And the tour of the maternity ward at Lutheran General."

My jaw tightens. I could punch him in the stomach right now.

"He's probably anxious about being a dad," I say. "Maybe he's kind of checked out? People do that when they're stressed."

My words are solely to comfort Elisabeth. Defending Bristowe's behavior sends the tang of vomit to the back of my throat. I rinse it down with some warm Earl Grey.

"He was so excited at first," she says. "He actually cried when I showed him the positive pregnancy test. We'd been trying for years. None of the fertility treatments were working. And then *she* happened." She pats her swollen belly. "Crazy how things work out, isn't it, Meadow?"

"So crazy." I polish the stainless steel oven doors before moving to the microwave that's built into the island. A plate of cookies and brownies is covered beneath a glass cloche a few feet away.

"Do you want some?" Elisabeth rises, grabbing a napkin before I can protest. "You can always tell how stressed I am by how many baked goods are in the house at any given time. Reed tells me to quit or he's going to gain weight. Guess he needs to watch his girlish figure. Here."

She hands me a cookie. Oatmeal raisin. The faint scent of cinnamon and brown sugar mix with lemon kitchen cleaner, but I take a bite and the thing practically melts in my mouth. Soft and chewy.

Baked with love.

Baby Mabry is so lucky to have Elisabeth as her mom. They haven't even formally met yet and already there's so much love in her eyes when she talks about her daughter.

"We should get coffee sometime," Elisabeth says. "Er, tea, I mean."

We chuckle. I've cleaned her house week after week, month after month, and she's never asked me to do anything outside these walls.

"I'd love some help decorating the nursery. If you're into that kind of thing," she adds. "Reed's been so busy . . ."

I read once that a person's home is a subconscious reflection of their true self, and I get it now. The signs were here all along—I just didn't want to see them. This house is all Elisabeth, curated and comforting and interesting. And the Reed parts? Those are found in the unfinished nursery. The leather-scented study he never uses because he prefers to work from his campus office. The barrage of leftovers filling their refrigerator because he's never home for dinner.

I never saw it before, but I suppose we're always seeing what we want to see.

"Sorry." Elisabeth chuckles. "I feel like I'm throwing all this stuff at you at once. I don't want you to feel obligated. Just thought it would be fun. Besides, I've never seen you in any color but bright yellow . . . Plus I think we introverts need to get out more, you know? I think it can make a person crazy being cooped up all the time."

Glancing at my uniform, I shrug. "You have a point."

"I'm really going to miss you when you're gone, Meadow," she says. "We should've done this a long time ago. Hung out."

"We should have," I agree.

"Saturday, ten AM, Bellisima Pastry and Tart on Hayworth," she says. "They have the *best* raspberry scones. I could eat a hundred of them. Then you could just ride with me to the baby shower after?"

"It's a date." I could nurture this friendship so easily. Elisabeth is normal, refreshing. I do wish we'd have forged our friendship a little sooner, but better late than never.

Besides, she's going to need some help when the baby comes.

She can't do this on her own. Alone all the time. Her husband off philandering.

She needs me.

26

"Meadow." Someone calls my name halfway between the Garrison and Montclair buildings. I'm almost late for class and I almost ignore them, but the tap on my shoulder and the tromp of footsteps on the pavement behind me tell me it isn't an option.

Turning, I find Thayer, slightly winded and adjusting his messenger bag.

"Hey," I say, walking toward Montclair Hall. "What's up?"

"You have a minute?"

Not really. "Sure."

He exhales, rubbing his palm along his jaw. "I think Lauren's cheating on me."

Ya think?

"Really?" I can play dumb with the best of them. "Why do you think that?"

"Something I saw. On her phone." His jaw tenses. "And the way she's been lately. It's all just adding up. And I keep thinking about what you said. About trust. Do you know anything, Meadow? Has she said anything to you?"

This is a fork in the road I never saw coming. And now I'm stuck, with only seconds to decide which direction I'm going to take and no time to analyze the immediate outcome.

"I love her so much," he says, eyes glassy. And I believe him. He wouldn't put up with all this bullshit if he didn't think he loved her. "I have to know who it is. I have to."

"Thayer . . ." I feign hesitation, but my mind is made up. I'm singing like a goddamned canary.

"Meadow." His hand rests on my shoulder. We're standing outside the main entrance of Montclair now.

"I'm late for class." I take a step.

He takes a step. "Please. You know something. I can tell. You know who it is."

"Even if I did . . ." I shrug, and say, " . . . it's not my place."

"Please. Tell me," he says, voice almost breaking. I justify what I'm about to do a dozen different ways, assuring myself it's the right thing. She doesn't deserve him. He deserves to be happy. But more than that, he deserves the truth.

Biting my lip, I glance away for a second. "Don't tell her I told you."

"Of course."

"It's Professor Bristowe." My heart kicks up a notch and I'm lightheaded. Is this a euphoric high or the flood of anxiety-rooted adrenaline coursing my body? Either way, it's done. There's no going back now.

"Bristowe?" His eyes flash dark. His teeth and his fists and his entire body clenches. When he drags his hand through his hair and tilts his head back, I feel compelled to stay and be there for him—but I have a presentation in two minutes.

"You going to be okay, Thayer?"

He doesn't answer. Instead, he turns and leaves, disappearing into a pack of baby-faced freshman guys headed toward the IT study lounge.

I bite my bottom lip to keep from smiling.

27

Lauren didn't come home for two days.

At first, I thought something happened to her—that Thayer lost his temper and she was lying lifeless in a ravine somewhere. But she was reading my text messages, which meant she was alive.

He probably told her everything. They probably fucking made up.

And now she's avoiding me.

The front door opens Friday, sending a shudder through the old house. I stay in bed, listening to the sounds outside my bedroom.

Lauren walking up and down the hall.

The spray of her shower.

The drip of her faucet as she brushes her teeth.

The drone of some annoying NPR podcast that quickly shifts to some dance-happy iHeartRadio station.

The wail of the teakettle in the kitchen.

The pop of the toaster as she heats her English muffin.

The clink of the silverware drawer as she retrieves a butter knife to spread her strawberry preserves.

It isn't until the front door opens and slams and her engine purrs to life that I feel it's safe to come out.

Funny how last month I felt so free here. Now it's become a makeshift prison. Our happy little home has become a land mine–filled desert and we're just tiptoeing around one another.

It didn't have to be this way.

It isn't my fault Lauren chose to be a home-wrecking whore.

I'm not sure when I'll see her again. Or the kind of words that will be exchanged. All I know is the nuke has been dropped and shit's about to get real.

28

Bellisima Pastry and Tart on Hayworth is exactly the quaint and cozy place I'd expect Elisabeth Bristowe to pick, and when I arrive, she's already nabbed us a corner table by the front window.

"Meadow!" She rises and waves for me to join her, and when I get closer, I see she's already ordered my tea as well as two raspberry scones.

"You didn't have to do this . . ." I hang my jacket on the back of my chair.

"My treat." Elisabeth sits, wearing a pleasant smile and tired, baggy eyes. She didn't sleep last night. "It's so nice to get out of the house." Yawning, she reaches for her coffee. "Can't seem to get comfortable anymore. Swear I'm getting bigger by the second."

"Don't be ridiculous. You look amazing," I say. And it's true. She has one of those perfect bodies . . . not too big, not too small. Not too short, not too tall. Pregnancy looks incredible on her.

I wonder if Reed ever takes a moment to tell her that? Probably not.

"You're sweet to say that." She takes another sip before checking her watch. "Am I a terrible person if I say I wish Reed's aunt wasn't throwing me this shower?" Placing her mug down, she adds, "I just feel like everyone's so phony at them, you know? Do people really want to take time out of a perfectly good Saturday and buy me stuff and sit around eating finger foods acting like they're having a good time?"

"Some people might?"

She laughs. "Yeah. Maybe. But I bet most people don't. It's just an obligation. I hate obligations. They suck all the fun out of everything."

"We're going to have a good time," I assure her as I break off a piece of my raspberry scone. It's hard. And I've never liked scones. Not a fan of raspberries either. But I eat it anyway.

"Oh, Reed is coming," she says. "Guess he was able to carve time out of his busy schedule to make an appearance. I told him he had no choice, though. It's his family. He should stop by and say hello. Take some of the heat off me. They all adore him anyway. They only like me because they have to."

"I doubt that."

She shrugs. "It's true. His family has never been crazy about me and I've never been able to figure out why. I've been nothing but nice to them since the day he brought me home."

"Some families are just like that. Cold and exclusive."

"It's a shame," she says. "My family was never that way. We made sure everyone felt welcome, and if we didn't like them, we'd wait until they left before we said anything."

Elisabeth laughs, sipping her coffee. And then her smile fades.

"Wish my mom could be here today," she says, glancing down at her untouched scone. "She loved baby showers."

I cup my hand over hers from across the table. "I'm sure she's here in spirit."

My attempt to comfort her is cliché and unoriginal, but I'm not sure what else can be said to a motherless woman who's about to become a mother herself. There are not enough words in the English language to make lemonade out of a rotten lemon.

"Anyway." Her hand retracts and she dabs a rogue tear from her left eye. "This should be a happy day."

"Exactly."

We finish our scones, chat about nursery colors—she's leaning toward peach—and the time flies as I suppose it does when two friends are truly enjoying one another's company. Within an hour, we arrive at the community center. Elisabeth offered to drive us both and bring me back to my car, but I insisted I follow.

She's already been too kind.

Pink-and-white streamers drape from the ceiling, twisted and taped so they hang just so, and a table in the back of the room is covered in rose-gold tissue paper anchored by a three-tier cake—white frosting and real flowers. Silver plates of cucumber sandwiches and pacifier-shaped cream cheese mints flank the sides as well as a bowl of ginger ale punch, which everyone is drinking out of champagne flutes.

It's sweet that Reed's aunt would do all of this for her . . . especially considering the fact that his family supposedly doesn't like her. But maybe with the recent death of her mother they felt obligated? And maybe that's what Elisabeth was really trying to say back at Bellisima? I'm sure the more we get to know one another, the more insight I'll glean. For the time being, I pop a mint into my mouth and ladle some punch into two champagne flutes.

A group of women, mostly older, circle Elisabeth, smiling and chatting, their hands on her belly. I can't see her face, but I imagine she's playing right along, pretending she's thrilled to be here, even if she isn't.

I love that she trusted me enough to be honest, to confess her little secret.

That is the true marker of a friendship.

Honesty. Zero secrets.

"Look who it is!" someone squeals from the crowd of ladies dressed in pastel dresses.

Everyone turns to the doorway where Reed stands, shit-eating grin and palms open as they flock to him to shower him in hugs and kisses and sweet sentiments about how much they've missed him.

Elvis has entered the building.

Elisabeth stands back. Forgotten. Abandoned.

I go to her, handing her a flute of punch and remaining at her side. "Wow. They really love him, don't they?"

She smirks, huffing through her nose. "This is how it is . . . every . . . single . . . time. They just love him. Don't we all, though?"

Reed's dimples and dark hair and pressed button-down and slim-cut khakis command the room, and each aunt or cousin he talks to has his full, undivided attention. And he's engaged. Like everything they're saying is fascinating.

Reed Bristowe has charisma down to a science.

And he has everyone fooled.

Eventually he makes his way to his wife, slipping his hand around the small of her back and leaning down to kiss her forehead. Her demeanor relaxes, softening like a kitten napping in the sun.

"Meadow." He finally notices me. "Hi. Wasn't expecting to see you here. Glad you could make it."

"I invited her," Elisabeth says. "We had tea this morning."

Reed nods, a pleased glint in his eye. I wonder how many times he's told her to get out of the house, to find friends.

Maybe I was low-hanging fruit, but I'm still glad she picked me.

A woman and her teenage daughter rush up to the two of them, stealing their attention, and I get edged out of the conversation. Taking a seat at a nearby table, I watch the Bristowes, wondering if Elisabeth has the slightest inkling that there's trouble in paradise or if Reed has the slightest intention of ending things with Lauren before the baby's born.

Together the two of them look like one of those perfect couples you see in the photo inserts of a brand-new picture frame. They smile big. They laugh with each other. Their body language is in sync. They look like they belong together, like they couldn't possibly belong to anybody else.

I think about what Lauren said to me once, about looking closely at perfect people and finding their cracks. And I imagine Reed's body covered in fault lines with offshoots into other fault lines, all of it hidden under his J.Crew uniforms.

Glancing up, I find Elisabeth lowering herself into the chair beside me.

"These things are awful, aren't they?" she asks, sliding me a small plate full of pacifier-shaped mints. "You seem bored. These are good, by the way. I can't stop eating them."

I take a pale green one and let it melt on my tongue. "I'm not bored."

"Don't lie." She laughs. "It's okay. I'm bored. But don't tell anyone." Elisabeth points toward the mountain of gifts piling up on a table in the corner. "How many breast pumps do you think I'm going to open today?"

I chuckle. "Two. Maybe three."

"My money's on four. Gut feeling." She pops another mint, moaning. "Why do these have to be so damn addictive?"

"Where's Reed?" I ask when I realize I don't see him anywhere. The legion of women worshipping the ground he walks on seems to have dissipated, separating themselves among the circular tables with floral centerpieces.

"Had to go grade papers or something." She lifts a brow, her tone flat. "I think he just didn't want to be the only guy here."

Right.

"Okay, everyone, we're going to start the games! Make sure you each have a pen. Let me know if you don't." Reed's aunt Char commands the room in her pink Chanel jacket with her diamond Chanel brooch and black Chanel flats.

And it makes sense now, what Elisabeth was saying earlier, about how they only pretend to like her for Reed's sake. Exhibit A? Char is loaded, and she threw Elisabeth a baby shower in a rundown, rent-by-the-hour community center.

At least the cake is fancy. She didn't cheap out there.

Aunt Char paces the front of the room, rising on her toes to see if anyone needs a pen. Her sleek silver hair is cut into a bob and she wears thick, black-rimmed glasses. A style all her own, just like Reed. Then again, she is the woman who raised him.

Someone passes us some sheets with a crossword puzzle of some kind, all the answers geared toward baby things. I don't know the first thing about babies, but I try my best and get half of the answers before the timer goes off.

Elisabeth was the first one done, but she didn't raise her hand. She wanted to give someone else the chance to win. She's always looking out for other people like that, always putting them first.

Someone should return the favor.

And that someone should be me.

29

A girl cannot live off raspberry scones and cucumber sandwiches alone. I need real sustenance. And that's exactly why I placed a to-go order at a real restaurant (that serves cheese curds and ranch dressing and burgers so juicy they drip down your chin when you take a bite) the second I left the baby shower.

Backroads Beerhouse is a hole-in-the-wall bar and grill on the far side of town, sandwiched between a strip club and a two-pump gas station with bars on the windows and signs all over stating they don't accept bills larger than a twenty.

It's why I felt so comfortable dressed in sweats, my hair piled on top of my head and my makeup washed off my face. Nobody really makes eye contact here. Everyone just faces the bar or stares into their beer or glues their beady eyes to whatever game is playing on one of the twelve TVs hanging around the restaurant.

I check in with the bartender, giving him my name, and he runs back to the kitchen, returning with Styrofoam containers in a plastic sack with a ticket stapled to the top.

"Thirteen dollars and twenty cents," he says.

I couldn't even buy a Taki martini for that. I huff, handing over my debit card. My mouth waters when the charbroiled scent of my angus bacon cheeseburger fills my nostrils.

I tip him 20 percent because my bank account is still rather robust, grab my order, and dash out to my car so I can make it home while the food is still warm.

Only when I'm pulling out of the parking lot, I spot a familiar Lexus pulling in, two shiny xenon headlights, a cute little blonde behind the wheel. Beside her is a man in a T-shirt and baseball cap.

And it isn't Thayer.

Oh no. It's Reed Bristowe.

The man who hours ago graced us with his presence at his wife's baby shower before dashing off to "grade papers."

I hate him.

I *hate* him.

And I hate her.

This has to stop.

Tomorrow, we're having words.

And unlike her, it's not going to be pretty.

30

I don't remember the last time I slept this hard. I'm guessing I was in some kind of burger-and-cheese-curds food coma coupled with the fact that I chased a Benadryl with a glass of wine. After everything that transpired yesterday, I was too worked up. I wanted to sleep, to close my eyes and exist in a world where Lauren and Reed and pregnant orphaned wives didn't exist.

Everything that happened after seven o'clock last night is a damn mystery, and I'm honestly okay with that this time.

The sound of cupboard doors opening and closing tells me Lauren's home. I'm not sure when she got back—if it was this morning or sometime last night. But she clearly knows I'm home and she's clearly not trying to keep the noise down.

It's almost as if she wants me to get out of bed, to face her.

My heart races. I feel a showdown coming on. I'm finally going to get a chance to say all the things I've been dying to say to her for weeks now. Tossing the covers off my legs and grabbing my phone—I want to record this—I trek to the hall and duck into my bathroom to freshen up before I face the stupid whore.

When I emerge, she's seated at the kitchen table, rosy mouth glued to the lip of her favorite tea mug as she stares out the window. I take heavier steps. She turns to face me.

"Morning," she says, voice chipper. And then she has the audacity to smile. This bitch is crazy. "Haven't seen you in days. What've you been up to?"

"I texted you the other day," I say, arms folded. "You read it and ignored me. I figured you've been avoiding me."

Her blue eyes rest on mine, lashes fluttering. "Why would I ignore you?"

I shrug. I have no idea if Thayer told her what I shared.

"I've been staying at Thayer's for a few days," she says. "He's helping me with that video for my grandmother's birthday."

So, they're still together . . .

"Okay." I grab one of my cheap white mugs from my cupboard and make myself a cup of Earl Grey. I'll be damned if I ever drink another caramel green tea almond milk piece-of-shit latte. "Did you guys go out Friday night?"

I already know the answer to this. I stalked her Insta and Facebook all night that night. Not a single picture was posted, not a single status was updated.

"We stayed in and got caught up on *Game of Thrones*," she says, yawning. "Thought we'd take a break from the bar scene. What'd you do?"

Before I get the chance to respond, both of our phones light up with some kind of chirping and vibrating alert that sends a shock to my heart and nearly knocks Lauren off her seat.

"God, I hate when they do that," she says, reaching for her phone and silencing it. "I wish we could opt out of this stupid campus security alert bullshit."

Unlike her, I actually read these things.

CAMPUS POLICE ARE INVESTIGATING A HOMICIDE WHICH TOOK PLACE SOMETIME AFTER ELEVEN PM SATURDAY EVENING. MONDAY CLASSES ARE CANCELED UNTIL WE CAN DETERMINE IF THIS IS A PUBLIC SAFETY THREAT.

"Jesus," I say. "Someone died last night on campus."

Lauren's gaze flicks to mine. "What? No way. Who?"

I shrug. "Doesn't say."

She grabs her phone, firing off text after text. Mine lights with an email notification. Margaret Blume.

"Is it true it's Reed Bristowe?" she writes, only she copied the entire English department. Students, faculty, deans.

Gripping the countertop's edge, I stabilize myself since the ground feels a little unsteady. Drawing in a deep breath, I hope to God Margaret doesn't know what she's talking about. She usually doesn't.

"Ohmygod." Lauren's hand flies to her mouth. She's trembling. "It's Reed Bristowe."

"Blume doesn't know what she's saying half the time," I say. "I'll believe it when I see—"

"Blume?" She shakes her head, blue eyes narrowing. "No. I got a text from someone who knows someone who found him. Somebody shot him, Meadow. They shot him in his office last night. He's *dead*."

My throat swells when I try to speak. There's a sharp sting in my stomach, like someone sucker punched me.

Lauren sobs. Her face buried in her palms. Shoulders heaving. She's trying to speak but I can't understand any of it.

I take a seat across from her before my legs give out.

Bristowe is dead.

Not just dead . . . murdered.

Somebody killed him.

I never knew it was possible to feel so many things at one time. Dumbstruck. Speechless. Angry. Sad.

Somehow numb on top of it all.

And what was he doing on campus around midnight last night? Who lured him there? Was someone with him? Did someone know he was going to be there? Who wanted him dead?

Too many questions. Not enough answers.

"Lauren," I say, clearing my throat.

She glances up, pretty crystalline eyes cloudy and bloodshot, lids swollen, and face ruddy. I've never seen her so . . . ugly.

"I know you were with him yesterday," I say.

She's quiet.

"I saw you two together. At Backroads," I say. Still kills me that she would go to a place like that, though I suppose if you're not wanting to be seen by your regular crowd . . . that'd be the place to go.

She sits a little straighter, sniffs. "Okay. We had a thing."

A *thing*?

"Let's call it what it is," I say before correcting myself. "What it *was*. An affair."

"Do we have to do this now?" She rises, her hands splayed on the table. For the first time, she looks at me with bitterness in her eyes and she speaks to me with contempt in her tone . . . like *I'm* the asshole here. "I know it was wrong. I don't need a lecture. The man is dead, Meadow."

"I'm not saying you killed him," I say. "But you were one of the last people to see him alive. You should probably go to the police and let them know."

It's the least she can do. For Elisabeth. And the baby. They need closure and answers and above all else, they deserve to know the truth.

"Good God, Meadow." Her voice is raised and her eyes are wild. "My fucking boyfriend just died, can I have a minute?"

"Your boyfriend? What about Thayer?"

"You know what I mean." Lauren's nose is wrinkled.

"Does Thayer know about your little sidepiece?"

"No. He knows nothing." Her words send a tingle reverberating through every fiber of my body.

He does know. I told him.

Did he follow them? Did he plan this out, waiting for the right moment to strike? Was this some kind of sick revenge fantasy brought to life?

I want to throw up.

If Thayer did this . . . Reed's blood is on my hands. Not in any real, tangible way. But for the rest of my life, I'll know I'm the one who pushed the first domino into the next one, setting off a chain reaction that led to someone's murder.

"I know you're sad. I know you're in shock and you're grieving, but we have to go to the police," I say. "You don't understand. Thayer knew. I told him."

Lauren's flushed complexion fades into white.

"I think Thayer killed Bristowe." I rise, reaching for her arm. "We have to go, Lauren. If he did this, you're not safe here."

I don't need two dead bodies on my conscience.

She jerks away from me. "I'm not going to the police. Not yet."

"Then you're crazy." Or maybe guilty . . .

"Just stop . . ." Lauren's eyes brim with tears again and she swats me away. "I *loved* him, Meadow."

In an instant, she's gone. Her bedroom door slams a few seconds later. The pop of the lock echoes in the hall.

Her phone lies on the kitchen table, exactly where she left it, the screen filled with messages. Everyone's talking. And everyone heard that it's Bristowe.

I'm about to walk away when her phone vibrates with a new message, this time from Thayer.

SORRY ABT YOUR PROF. I KNOW HOW MUCH HE MEANT 2 U. . .

I take a picture of it with my phone.

Lauren can stay here, crying tears into her pillow for the rest of the day, but I'm going to the police.

31

I'd hoped they'd let me talk to the lead detective on the case—whose name I've learned is Lee Caldwell, but it appears they've placed me with some paper-pushing underling with a bad knee and a wheeze when she exhales.

I can only hope nothing gets lost in translation. I've never seen anyone write slower than Rhonda here, and she doesn't seem to be taking everything down.

"So Thayer knew that Lauren was cheating, but Lauren didn't know Thayer knew," I say.

"Right," she says, wheezing. "You've already said that."

I know. I've said it at least three times. But I didn't see her write it down.

"And do you have proof that the boyfriend knew that the girlfriend was cheating?" She places her pen down, peering over her glasses. I don't even think she finished writing her last sentence. Something's going to get mislaid here.

Typical government employee. Only here for the pension.

"No," I say. Her question is dumb. "I told you. He ran into me on campus and asked if I knew anything. I told him what I knew. How would I have proof? It was a conversation . . ."

"It's just a question, ma'am." I don't like her tone. And I'm twenty-two. Hardly a ma'am. *She's* the ma'am. "No need to get worked up."

Taking a deep breath and forcing myself to smile, I try to come at this from a different angle. "It's just that I can't help but notice that you're not writing everything down."

Rhonda's mouth draws into a slow side smirk. "These are my personal notes. Everything's being recorded."

She points to the ceiling, where a microphone hangs from a loose tile. Oh.

"Okay, so you said the two of them had a contentious relationship," she says, reading her notes. "Did you ever witness any physical altercations? See any markings or bruises?"

"No," I say. "But Thayer kind of . . . stalked her from time to time. She'd mentioned that to me. So did her friend, Tessa. He once showed up at our place because he didn't see her car at the barre studio. He knew when she worked out. He had her schedule memorized."

"It's not uncommon to memorize your significant other's schedule," she says, as if I didn't know. "Did he ever harass her while he 'stalked' her?"

"I'm not sure."

"Technically stalking includes harassment," she says. "Did Lauren ever tell him to stop following her?"

"I'm sure. They fought all the time. Breaking up, getting back together," I say. "I witnessed it firsthand a couple of times."

"It happens." She chuckles, shaking her head. "Sounds like my daughter and her boyfriend."

This isn't funny.

"I think we've got all we need," she says, pushing herself up and hunching over the table. She checks the black-and-white clock on the wall.

"I was just getting started," I say, retrieving my phone. "Look. Look what he sent her this morning. It's cryptic."

Peering through the bifocal section of her glasses, she reads the message. "You can't infer anything from this."

"Okay, but you don't understand the rage, the hatred I saw in his eyes when I told him about Lauren and Bristowe," I say. "And now Bristowe's dead and Thayer's offering his condolences? And don't you think it's odd that I saw Lauren and Reed together and then hours later he's dead? What if Thayer was following them?"

"We're going to look into him," Rhonda says with a sigh. She acts like she's doing me a favor, like I'm inconveniencing her. And I get it. I know I didn't come here with hardcore, irrefutable, tangible evidence. I understand I presented her with a theory rooted in assumptions and pure speculation. But every shred of me knows Thayer had something to do with it.

He's the only one who would've wanted to hurt the two of them. Physically and emotionally.

"Thanks for coming in, Meadow," she says. Rhonda reaches into her pocket and hands me Lee Caldwell's card. "Lee will be in touch with you if he has any questions."

Rhonda walks me out to the lobby of the police station before waddling over to the receptionist and stealing a piece of candy from a bowl on her desk. The thought of going home makes my stomach heavy, and I start to tremble, erratically. Like I've been doing all day. I can't control it. It's like the fear and anxiety and shock are all bubbling to the surface, trying to get out.

Getting into my car a minute later, I silence the radio and let the engine warm.

Elisabeth.

I back out of the parking spot and drive east on Mayfair Avenue, toward the Bristowe house. And I don't need to call first because we're friends and friends drop in on each other, especially in times of need.

And she needs me.

She needs me now more than she's ever needed me before.

32

Aunt Char opens the door in sunglasses, as if the Bristowe house wasn't already dark enough. Every curtain is drawn. Every light switched off—save for the one above the kitchen sink and a lamp in the living room.

"Can I help you?" she asks, twisting the black pearls around her wrinkled neck.

The darkness seeps out of the house, wrapping me in an ominous embrace. I can feel the weight of Elisabeth's sadness already.

"I'm a friend of Elisabeth's," I say, holding a brown paper bag of raspberry scones I picked up on the way here. I doubt she's in the mood to eat anything right now, but it's the thought that counts.

She eyes me up and down, maybe deciding she recognizes me from the baby shower yesterday, and then she lets me in. A couple of police officers chat in the kitchen and Char tells me Elisabeth is upstairs in her room and offers to "fetch" her for me.

I wait in the foyer and a moment later, Char returns, Elisabeth in tow. Her hair has been brushed, pulled tight in a low ponytail, and her nose is red, raw.

"Meadow," she says, gripping the stair rail. When she hits the landing, she shuffles toward me, wrapping me in an embrace, though I should be the one holding her.

"Elisabeth, I'm so sorry," I say.

"How did you know?"

"Everybody knows," I say. "The whole campus knows."

She breathes me in and lets me go. "It doesn't feel real."

"It doesn't." Our eyes hold. "But you're going to get through this."

The house is empty, save for the cops and Aunt Char, and I know now more than ever that I'm all she's got.

"Are you hungry?" I rub her arms. "When was the last time you ate?" Steering her toward the dining room, I pull out a seat. "Stay here. I'll make you a sandwich. You might not want to eat right now, but I bet that baby does."

Five minutes later, I return with a turkey sandwich, a container of vanilla yogurt, a napkin, spoon, and a glass of milk, and then I take the spot beside her.

"Thank you, Meadow. You didn't have to do this." She lifts the sandwich to her mouth, taking a reluctant bite. I doubt she tastes it.

"How long is Char staying?" I ask.

She shrugs. "She hasn't said much of anything to me. I've asked her to handle the . . . final arrangements."

The sandwich falls on her plate and she dabs her eyes with a paper napkin printed with pink stars and purple flowers.

"Who's going to take care of you after this?" I ask. "Who are you going to call when you need something?"

Elisabeth leans against the tall back of the wooden dining chair, forehead wrinkled. "I haven't thought that far ahead."

"Do you have anyone who can stay with you? A cousin or something?"

Biting her trembling lip, she shakes her head. "No one that I'd feel comfortable asking to inconvenience."

Rolling my eyes at her self-deprecation, I place my hand over hers. "Me. I'll do it."

"What?"

"I'll move in. I'll help you with everything. I'll clean the house, I'll run your errands. I'll take you to your ultrasounds and birthing classes, and—"

"Meadow, you can't," she says. "You have school. And work. And I couldn't do that to you. My burdens are not yours."

"It wouldn't be a burden," I say. I have enough money in my account that I don't even need to work at Sparkle Shine Cleaning Co. anymore. "I'll still go to class and everything. I'll just be here when I'm not there. You'll have me at your complete disposal."

"You are way too generous."

"I want to do this for you," I say, chin tucked and tone steady. "Let me do this for you."

Elbow on the table, she rests her chin on her hand, staring ahead at a portrait of General Washington hanging on the dining room wall.

"I know you don't want the help," I say. "But you need it. And believe me when I say, I'm happy to do this."

Our eyes hold and her hazel eyes tear. "I'm not exactly in a position to say no, am I?"

She half laughs.

"Nope," I say, shoving her plate closer and peeling the lid from her yogurt. "Someone has to stay here and make sure you don't waste away."

I hand her the spoon next, and she accepts it with a trembling hand.

"I don't know who would want to hurt him, Meadow," she says, voice cracked. "Everybody loved him. Anyone who knew him knew he was about to become a father. Who would do this?"

There's a heaviness in my chest, one I imagine barely compares to the one in hers right now.

The world is cruel.

And there's not much worse than being a pregnant widow.

"It's tragic." My words are a forced, breathy whisper. I can't tell her about Thayer . . . not yet. Not until I know for sure and not until she's stronger, emotionally and physically. "Listen, you need to eat. And I'm going to run home and get my things. Call me if you need anything, do you understand?"

Elisabeth dips her spoon into her yogurt, leaving it there. "I will."

I show myself out, and on the drive to Lauren's, I practice exactly what I'm going to say to her when I get there.

33

Lauren's car is in the driveway but the house is silent. As far as I know, she's still in her room, crying thick crocodile tears and ignoring the rest of the world.

On the way here, I stopped and picked up an oversized suitcase, something big enough to hold all of my things. Ripping off the tags, I hoist it onto my bed and begin yanking clothes off hangers and tossing them in. There's no time for folding.

When I'm finished shoving my clothes and shoes and bags together, I head to my bathroom and walk away with an armful of shampoo and a couple of travel totes' worth of skin and makeup products.

Everything fits. My entire life in a zippered bag with wheels.

I slide my computer into my purse last, wrapping the charging cord around my palm before tucking it into a side pocket.

"What are you doing?" Lauren stands in my doorway, leaning, yawning. Her hair is a mess, face puffy. She's been sleeping.

"I'm moving out." I stand tall.

Her arms fold. "Why?"

"I don't feel comfortable being here anymore."

"Okay, now you're overreacting," she says. "Thayer would never hurt anyone."

"This isn't just about Thayer."

Lauren's mouth presses flat. "So you don't feel comfortable living here because of *me*?"

"That too." I drag my suitcase off the bed and wheel it toward the doorway, but she doesn't budge.

"Should we talk about this or something?" she asks.

"My mind is made up." I motion for her to step aside. "I don't know what happened to Bristowe, but I know what my gut tells me. And it's that one of you has something to hide, and I want nothing to do with this."

"You realize how insane you sound right now, don't you?" The bitch laughs at me. She's only trying to provoke me into an argument so she can convince me to stay, so she can get her way. I've seen her do it dozens of times with Thayer, only I never realized what she was doing all those times. Not until now. She's a manipulative, cunning, slippery little whore.

I say nothing. All those things I practiced in the car on the way here? I keep them to myself. She's smarter than I've given her credit for, and I'm not ready to play my hand yet.

So I leave.

I leave the pretty house and the pretty roommate and the pretty life I'd come to love.

I know now that none of it was real.

I know now that *this* is real—life and death and heartache and pregnant widows.

And I want to live in the real world again.

34

Classes resumed yesterday and as of today, Reed Bristowe's murder was officially confirmed in a campus-wide email. It's an ongoing investigation. Rumor is he was shot in the back—which I already knew because Elisabeth told me one quiet night by the fireplace.

Other rumors are that he was poisoned, that his throat was slit, or that he overdosed on heroin. I keep the truth to myself. I don't want to accidentally thwart the police's ongoing efforts.

I find a spot in the back row at World Lit, watching the door to see if Lauren walks in. There's a TA in the front, messing with the projector. She's baby faced and clearly has no idea what she's doing. The poor thing is shaking like a leaf and I wonder if it's because she's scared or if she's shaken by the death of her beloved colleague.

A folded *Meyer State Herald* lies abandoned on the seat beside me, the headline reading **CAMPUS MURDER— WHAT YOU HAVEN'T HEARD**. Since when did the *Herald* become *The National Enquirer*? Grabbing the paper, I scan the article. It's all hearsay mixed with speculation in a way that makes it seem legit. Some of the facts, I can confirm—he was discovered by a night guard who was making his rounds. He was wearing a T-shirt and a ball cap. He was shot in the back. There were no witnesses as far as I know, but the article is begging anyone who knows something to come forward immediately.

At the bottom of the article, in italicized print, are the words: *For tips and corrections, please email Editor-in-Chief Emily Waterford at ewaterford@meyerrstateherald.edu.*

I almost choke on my spit.

Emily Waterford.

The clock above the projection screen says class should've started five minutes ago, but the TA doesn't seem any closer to being ready than she was before. I shove my pen and notebook into my bag and make the decision to cut class. Outside, I sprint across campus, heading straight for the *Herald* headquarters on the south side.

The directory at the entrance shows Emily's office on the fourth floor. 41A.

I blink and I'm there and I don't remember if I took the elevator or the stairs, all I know is I have to talk to her immediately and her door is closed.

Lifting my fist to knock, the door swings open before I get a chance to begin. A petite girl with shiny auburn hair, a polka-dot shirt, and a pencil skirt jumps back.

"Oh. Hello," she says, one hand over her chest and another gripping an empty coffee mug. "Can I help you?"

"Are you Emily Waterford?"

Her eyes go from side to side. I probably look like a crazy-eyed, breathless psychopath, but I don't care.

"I am," she says slowly, carefully. The tiniest crow's feet flank her pretty green eyes and she speaks with one of those young, baby-doll voices.

"What do you know about 47 Magpie Drive?" I ask.

I'd searched for her in the campus student directory once, coming up empty-handed. But it makes sense now. She's staff. Not a student.

And she's been here all along, hiding in plain sight. I just didn't look hard enough.

"I used to live there," she says. "Only for a few months. I was waiting to close on a house. Why?"

"So you know Lauren Wiedenfeld."

Her mouth twists at the side. "No. Don't think that I do? Why?"

"She lives there," I say with as much conviction as I can muster. "You were her roommate."

Emily releases a nervous titter. "Is this some kind of practical joke? I have no idea what you're talking about. Did Kevin set me up?"

She glances down the hall, half expecting to see someone.

"Lauren's parents own that house," I say. "Her brother lived there before. And she's lived there for the last four years. She said she's never had a roommate, but I found some mail with your name on it under one of the beds."

Emily frowns. "I think you're confused."

She doesn't think I'm confused—she thinks I'm crazy. I see it in her eyes, in the way she's been taking tiny steps away from me like I wouldn't notice.

"I moved out in early December," she says. "And Silver Hill Properties owns that house. Maybe you've heard of them? They own three-fourths of the rentals in Monarch Falls? Billboards everywhere you look?"

"Silver Hill?"

"Check the assessor's site," she says. "Silver Hill is the property management company, and they're owned by Janet Silver-Hill and Robert Hill. Trust me, I used to be a fact-checker. I know these things. And now that I think about it, I remember they said they had someone lined up for January. That's the only reason they let me out of my lease early. Someone was moving in on the seventh, a week before classes started. Don't ask me why I remember that."

"It's just . . . I moved in there . . . and the girl said she'd lived there for years and never had a roommate," I say.

"She lied." Emily shrugs. "People lie all the time about stupid stuff for no reason. Anyway, is that all you wanted to ask me?"

I nod. "Yeah. Sorry for all the freaking out. I'm just . . . trying to piece some things together."

"Check the assessor's site," she says as she steps out of her office. I move out of the way and she closes the door. "That's what I'd do. And then call the property management company. They won't be able to give you names, but if you ask the right questions, you might find what you're looking for. I speak as a veteran journalist."

She gifts me with a wink before strutting down the hall, her chunky heels clunking on the tile.

Taking a seat on a nearby bench, I slide my phone out of my bag and search 47 Magpie Drive on the Monarch Falls Assessor's page. Sure enough, Emily was right. Silver Hill Properties is the listed owner. Jay and Suzette Wiedenfeld are nowhere to be found.

I call the front office of Silver Hill next.

"Silver Hill Properties, this is Samantha. How can I help you?" a pleasant voice answers.

"Hi, I'm interested in one of your properties," I say as cordially as I possibly can. Heat flashes through my body and I'm trembling again. Little earthquakes that won't stop. "47 Magpie Drive is the address."

"Sure. Two seconds." The click of keys in the background are followed with, "Okay, found it. All right, 47 Magpie Drive is currently in contract through July thirty-first of this year. I'd be happy to arrange a tour for you if you're interested? Or I can have someone call you with some similar options. Is there something specific you're looking for? Or what did you like about it? The neighborhood? Forest Hills is one of our more popular locations. It's great for families, too. Very quiet. Safe."

"Can I let you know?" I ask.

"Of course . . ." she starts to say something else, but I hang up before she can coerce my contact information. Besides, I don't think I could speak if I tried. With my elbows on my knees and my head in my hands, I breathe in and breathe out, trying to understand what this means.

Lauren subleased the apartment through July.

Her parents never owned it.

All of this was a lie.

But . . . why?

35

I'm elbow deep in oven mitts, attempting to drain the pasta I've boiled for Elisabeth's dinner tonight, when my phone skids across the counter, a local number flashing across the screen.

Leaving the steaming pasta in the colander, I yank off a mitt and answer by the fourth ring. "Hello?"

"Meadow Cupples, this is Lee Caldwell, Monarch Falls police," he says. "Was wondering if you had some time tonight to come in and talk?"

Finally.

They're taking me seriously.

"Of course," I say, pacing the Bristowe kitchen. Elisabeth is upstairs in bed, where she's been spending most of her time this week. I ran to the library yesterday, checking out dozens of books for her because all she does anymore is watch TV. Though I'm not entirely sure she's actually watching it—I think she likes the sound. Makes her feel like she's not alone. "Give me a half hour?"

Caldwell isn't at all what I expected. He's younger, maybe mid- to late twenties? Full head of blond hair that he wears long enough that he can tuck it behind his ears and it curls on the ends. Baseball-player build.

Disarming mannerisms. He takes his time, speaks slowly, and dedicates his full attention to everything I say or do.

He's a thinker. Like me. I can tell.

Lee Caldwell is no dummy.

"Appreciate you coming in today, Meadow." He sits across from me, elbows on the table, hunched forward. It's like we're just a couple of pals.

"Of course. Anything I can do to help," I say. "Elisabeth Bristowe is a very close friend of mine. I'm just heartbroken for her."

Pushing a hard breath through his nose, he covers his mouth with his hands. "Mm-hmm."

"Ask me anything. I'll tell you whatever you need to know."

Lee nods. "We've got a lot to cover tonight."

Good. He's thorough. I like that.

"I'd like to start with Lauren Wiedenfeld," he says, tapping his pen cap on the table. "So she's your roommate."

"Yes. Was. I moved out recently."

"And how long have you known her?" he asks.

"Since February twelfth," I say.

"And how did you meet?"

"She posted an ad on the Tiger Paw Campus Portal looking for a roommate. I was looking for a place to stay. We met up and hit it off." These questions are redundant. I went over these details days ago with Rhonda, but I'm sure he's looking for inconsistencies. That's what they do. They look for little holes in your story and that's where they know to start digging.

I've got nothing to worry about, though. The truth is always consistent.

"So you like her?" he asks.

"*Liked*," I correct him. "We were friends. I found out about Bristowe, started distancing myself from her."

"Distancing yourself how? Why?"

The Perfect Roommate

"We just stopped hanging out," I say. "Avoiding each other at home. I didn't agree with her sleeping with a married man. I didn't want to be associated with that."

"Let's go back to when you two were friends," he says it like it was years ago, not weeks ago. "Tell me more about how you felt about her. Initially."

His question is odd, but I answer anyway. "She was nice and welcoming. Introduced me to her family . . . her friends . . . her boyfriend. We got along perfectly."

"Is it fair to say you idolized her?"

I cock an eyebrow. "I don't know about *idolizing* her . . ."

"You looked up to her, then."

Shaking my head, I say, "I'm sorry. What does that have to do with Bristowe's murder?"

"You dressed like her," he says. His statement catches me off guard. Obviously he's been talking to Lauren.

"She gave me her old clothes." I'm quick to land on my feet.

"Wore the same perfume," he adds.

"I liked the way it smelled." She must have been snooping through my things—I thought I'd kept the bottle of Versace perfume well hidden.

"You shared hairdressers, even had your hair highlighted like hers," he says.

"At her insistence." I squint at him, trying to steady the outraged tremble in my voice.

"If I were to look in your phone right now, at your music, would it be the same music she listened to?" he asks.

"Friends share music all the time," I say.

"You were preoccupied with her relationship with Thayer Montgomery," he says.

I scoff. "Preoccupied? Hardly."

"You were constantly asking her about him," he says. "Asking her friends about him. Anytime you had Thayer alone, you'd try and talk to him about their relationship. Prying questions. You tried to break them up on several occasions. You wanted them apart."

My jaw drops. "You have it all wrong."

He speaks as if these ridiculous claims are hard, cold facts. And he doesn't flinch, doesn't blink. I had him all wrong. He's not friendly or personable, he's not your friendly, neighborhood guy next door, and he's definitely not on my side.

Lee Caldwell is a professional manipulator, skilled at planting seeds and harvesting information, fertile soil or not.

"So none of these things are true?" He lifts a brow and leans back in his chair. He thinks I'm deranged, unstable.

"They're true, but you're making me sound like I was obsessed with Lauren's life, and I wasn't," I say. "When you put all those things together, I know the kind of picture it paints, but you're wrong."

"Is it true you were in possession of a firearm?" he asks next, ignoring everything I just said.

Fucking Lauren.

"I took it from my mother's boyfriend," I said. "I was going to throw it in the Monarch Falls lake. I don't even know how to shoot a gun."

His hand covers his mouth once more and he glances down, at the notebook in front of him. From where I'm seated, I can't make out his handwriting. It's tiny and sloppy.

"What kind of gun was it, Meadow?" he asks.

I shrug. "I told you, I don't know anything about guns."

Glock. It was a Glock. I remember now.

"I think it was a Glock," I say.

His lips flatten and his gaze locks on mine. "And you still have this gun in your possession?"

Shit.

I left it under my mattress at Lauren's. Completely spaced it off when I was packing.

"It should be at Lauren's," I say. "It was hidden. Under the mattress in the room I rented."

"We'll have someone retrieve it," he says. "Ballistics will need to take a look at it."

"That's perfectly fine," I say. "It's all yours. I don't even want it back."

"Can you tell me about Saturday night? Where you were . . . what you did?" He's trying to establish my alibi now.

"I stayed home," I say. "I got dinner and stayed home and took a Benadryl and drank a glass of wine and went to bed early."

"What time?" he asks.

"I don't know? Seven, eight?"

His mouth turns down at the corners.

"I know most college students don't go to bed at seven o'clock on a Saturday night, but I'd had a long week and I just wanted to sleep," I say.

"Can anybody corroborate that you were home all evening?" he asks. "Did you talk to anyone? Anyone stop by?"

I shake my head. "I told you. I was alone. And I was sleeping."

He jots something down. The silence between us is weighted, intolerable, and my stomach is nothing but knots.

"Did you check into Thayer Montgomery's alibi?" I ask.

Lee glances up. "His sister was able to verify that he was in Waverly Heights at a family dinner."

"What about Lauren?" I ask.

"She admitted she was with the victim earlier in the day, but they went their separate ways sometime after nine o'clock. We have text messages that confirm that."

"I'm sorry, I'm just really confused right now," I say, half chuckling. "It sounds like you think *I* had something to do with this?"

He says nothing, but I know what this is about.

Lauren found out I came in here and pointed a finger at her and Thayer, so she marched in here and pointed one right back. She painted me as obsessed with her, jealous. Unhinged. She made me look crazy, like someone capable of doing something so heinous. And then she told them I had a gun.

Someone knocks on the door, stealing Lee's attention, and he folds the leather portfolio containing his yellow legal pad. "I think I've got enough for now. I'll be in touch if I need anything more. You stick around town, okay?"

So that's that.

I'm officially a person of interest.

36

I sit in Elisabeth's driveway for the better part of twenty minutes, still shaking, replaying my time with Lee over and over in my mind.

How do I tell her the police think I had something to do with her husband's murder? How do I explain that he was cheating on her, I knew about it, and I never told her? A true friend would've said something, but I only ever wanted to protect her.

Resting my forehead against the steering wheel, I kill the engine and step out onto the paved walkway to the back door. It's late now, the house is dark, and Elisabeth is probably in bed. The doctors gave her a light sedative, something safe for her to take to help her sleep. And that's all she's been doing. Sleeping the days away. She told me when she's asleep, it's the only time she can be with Reed. When she wakes up, it's like he died all over again.

Twisting my key in the lock of the back door, I tiptoe inside, kicking off my shoes and maneuvering through the darkened kitchen. Not only does this house feel like death, it looks like death, too.

I fix myself a sandwich and a glass of juice, eating at the island.

I'm going to have to tell Elisabeth, at least before the police do. I don't want her to find out that way, and I want a chance to explain myself. She'll probably kick me out, but I would, too. It's going to hurt knowing that I kept this from her.

There's enough money in my account to get me by through the end of summer if I spend carefully, but if I can't land a short-term rental,

I'm going to have to stay at a hotel, and that's going to eat through everything I've got left.

I'll end up right back where I was. Broke and homeless.

Everything I own in my back seat.

Finishing my supper, I pad upstairs, passing Elisabeth's door. The flicker of TV light illuminates the bottom, but it's hard telling if she's awake or not. Either way, Reed's funeral is almost here and I'm not going to bother her with this yet.

In two days, she buries her husband.

The day after that? I'll tell her everything I know.

37

Elisabeth wakes at a quarter past three in the morning. I know because I hear the hum of the water pipes, the soft scuff of her swollen footsteps up and down the hall.

I also know this because I haven't slept since my head hit the pillow. There's too much adrenaline coursing through me from Caldwell's interrogation, too many unanswered questions. At this rate, I might as well stay up the rest of the day. Anything is better than lying here, wallowing in a puddle of the unknown.

Climbing out of bed, I decide to check on her, see if she needs anything. I'm sure Reed's impending funeral is weighing heavy, filling her every thought.

But she has me.

I'll get her through this.

The two of us—together.

Padding down the dim hallway, I find her door closed and the flicker of TV light at the bottom—same old—only the sound of her voice rises above the drone of the infomercial playing in the background.

She's talking to someone.

"We haven't even buried him yet and already you're asking about this?" Her words are rushed, pointed. Her shadow momentarily obstructs the pale TV light at the bottom of the door before moving on. From the sound of her footsteps, she's pacing the room. "You know exactly what we agreed on. Don't call me again. Not until I say you can."

I'm frozen, wondering if I'm sleepwalking, dreaming. Wondering if everything I just heard was a product of an exhausted, overtaxed imagination.

Creeping back to my room, I bury myself under the covers, trying to make sense of Elisabeth's words. By the time the sun comes up, I surrender to the fact that I can't explain any of that away.

Someone called her, wanting something. Something they could only get if Reed was dead. And she told them not to call her again until she said they could. The only logical explanation? Money. Life insurance. Inheritance. Something along those lines.

Maybe Elisabeth knew about his affair? Maybe she wanted retribution and to be set for life and this was the only way? It would make sense, especially with the baby. Everything would go to the two of them, guaranteed. And anything Reed would've inherited from his loaded Aunt Char would go to the baby eventually as well.

Sitting up in my bed, I drag my hands down my face and exhale. This is bad. This is really fucking bad.

I'm going to have to talk to Lauren, I'm going to have to extend an olive branch, and we're going to have to stop accusing each other long enough to get justice for Reed Bristowe, philandering asshole that he was.

And this is the only way we'll be able to clear our names.

38

"You told them I was crazy," I say to Lauren later that Monday morning.

We decided to meet on campus, someplace neutral. She chose the park bench outside Griffin Hall, which is the farthest point from the English department. This area is dead since Griffin is under renovation, and while there's a student body of almost twenty thousand roaming around, out here, it's just us.

"I didn't make you sound crazy, I just told them what I knew, what I'd witnessed. They inferred the rest," she says. "*You* told them Thayer killed Reed."

"How did you know I had a gun?" I ask.

"Please." Lauren rolls her swollen eyes. She hasn't stopped crying over him, probably in days. "You went through my shit all the time. I can't count how many times I found things moved, products dwindling quicker than I could use them."

"You're exaggerating."

"Still. I know you were in my room. The only reason I went into yours was because I couldn't find something and I thought maybe you'd taken it," she says. "Then I found your gun."

"It isn't mine actually. It belongs to my mom's boyfriend. I was going to get rid of it," I say. "I forgot it was there, honestly."

She says nothing, just like Caldwell. Lauren doesn't believe me either.

"You were obsessed with Thayer and me, though," she says. "Even Tessa noticed it."

"I wasn't obsessed." I cross my legs and stare toward campus. We should be making peace but instead we're bickering, pulling on threads, and taking digs and getting nowhere. "It's complicated."

"I bet." Lauren huffs.

"You lied about the house. Your parents didn't own it. You were subletting."

Her head tilts and her brows rise and her mouth curls at one side. "Yeah. I was."

"Why did you make up that whole story about your monthly stipend and your GPA?"

Lauren re-crosses her legs, staring forward and hooking her hands around her knees. "I was living with Thayer before." She clears her throat. "We got into a fight. I moved out to prove a point. I didn't want a year lease, just something to get me through the end of the year. I found the house. Moved in. Realized I couldn't afford it, so I decided to get a roommate. The sublease didn't allow for that, so I thought it was easier just to say my parents owned the house. I didn't want to scare you away or make you think I was shady." She turns to me. "I liked you, Meadow. I liked you from the moment I met you."

I offer her a tight-lipped smile. It's sad that it's come to this. We could've been great friends. We could've had a friendship that spanned careers and decades and continents.

But she lied. She lied about everything.

One more question before I put a stop to this juvenile backbiting. "Why did you have my necklace?"

"What necklace?"

"The sterling silver heart with my initials," I say. "I knocked over your purse once and that spilled out."

Her eyes widen. "Oh! That. I found it on the floor in the hallway one day when I was leaving for class. Didn't want it to get lost, so I threw it in my bag. Meant to give it to you. Guess I forgot."

Exhaling, I accept her explanation for the time being, if only because it's undeniably plausible and I have bigger fish to fry. "All right, let's just get to the point here."

Lauren angles her body toward mine.

"I've been staying with Elisabeth Bristowe," I say, watching the shock register on her face. "She's actually a friend of mine, and I've been taking care of her this past week. Anyway, I overheard something in the middle of the night—a phone call. Someone called to ask her about something. It sounded like money . . . and then she told them not to contact her until she said they could. Lauren, I think Elisabeth paid someone to kill her husband."

She glances away, swiping a tear from her right eye. I wait for her to say something, to tell me I'm being ridiculous, that my theory makes no sense.

Hell, I want her to prove me wrong.

I don't want to believe Elisabeth is capable of something so vile and beneath her.

"He was worth a lot of money," Lauren finally breaks her silence. "Millions. He told me once. When his parents died, everything was put in a trust that he couldn't access until his thirty-fifth birthday . . . next year."

She whispers the words I didn't want to hear.

"We have to go to the police," I say. "Immediately."

Lauren turns to face me, shoulders slumped, defeated. "Yeah. You're right."

I rise, slipping my bag over my shoulder. We need to leave. Now.

"We should stop at Thayer's on the way," she says. "It's only fair we present with a united front since you accused us both of having something to do with this."

"Fine."

I follow her to a church parking lot across the street, climbing into the passenger seat of her Lexus and buckling my seatbelt as she taps out a text message to let him know we're on our way.

We don't speak on the drive to Thayer's, but I'm breathing easier. Closure is just around the corner.

Everything makes sense.

And soon, this nightmare will be over.

39

"He's not answering." Lauren sighs as we wait in the parking lot of Thayer's apartment building. "Texts or calls. We're going to have to knock."

Climbing out of her car and up the stairs to the second level, I follow her to apartment 2D and stand back as she balls her manicured fist and pounds on the door. The muffled sound of some Pantera song blasts on the other side of the door, which explains why he didn't hear his phone.

Lauren knocks once more, nostrils flaring and lips pursed. She's just as anxious as I am to get to the police station. The music dies and the door swings open.

Thayer's eyes widen and his form fills the doorway. He's surprised to see us—me especially.

I'm pretty sure I'm on his shit list right now, and understandably so. I went to the police and told them I thought he murdered someone, and now I have the nerve to show up at his place? My posture wilts as I imagine the look he's going to give me, but I suck in a deep breath and force myself to do the right thing.

"What's this?" he asks, brows meeting as his gaze is directed at me.

"Didn't you get my text?" Lauren asks, fidgeting.

He pulls his phone from his back pocket, swiping his thumb across the screen. "Now."

She rolls her eyes. "We need to go to the police. Meadow thinks Bristowe's wife had something to do with his death. She, um, heard something. I thought we should all go together?"

Thayer turns his attention to me, drawing in a hard breath, examining me. Maybe I owe him an apology, but now's not the time.

"I think Elisabeth paid someone to kill her husband," I say. "I heard her on the phone in the middle of the night. It sounded like someone was asking for money and she talked about an agreement and waiting."

"You're sure?" he asks. And he has a right to ask. My track record with assuming things isn't the greatest.

I nod. "Positive. I mean, it's not like she admitted to anything, but I think the police should check into this."

Thayer steps out of the doorway, glancing at Lauren. They exchange a look that I can't read.

"What did you hear, exactly?" he asks, one hand cocked on his left hip as he studies me. Already, I can tell he doesn't want to believe me. That or he simply doesn't want anything to do with me.

"She was on the phone," I begin, "and she said something like 'we haven't even buried him yet and already you're asking for this? Don't call me again until I say you can.'"

Thayer drags a hand across his face before glancing toward the distance. "That could mean anything."

"I know." My hand clasps over my heart. "I know it could mean anything. But what if it doesn't? Shouldn't we at least tell the police?"

Lauren's gaze darts between us. I'm not used to her being so quiet and reserved around either of us, but then again, she's been through the wringer this week. The man she loved was brutally murdered. That'd be enough to send anyone into a silent tailspin.

"Lauren?" Thayer turns his attention to her.

"We should go to the police," she says. Her lips press into a straight line as she pauses. "All of us."

His jaw flexes as he contemplates, and a moment later he says, "Just . . . give me a minute to shower."

"Really?" I lift a brow. He looks fine to me. Maybe his clothes are a little wrinkled and his mussed hair could use a comb, but last I checked, the police station didn't have a dress code.

"Twenty minutes," he says. "And then we'll go."

40

I follow Lauren into Thayer's apartment, and we take a seat in the living room on a saggy, beer-stained sofa positioned across from a seventy-inch TV with at least three different gaming consoles arranged beneath it. A *Rocky IV* poster hangs behind me and the curtains are drawn tight.

I'm not sure why, but I was always under the impression that Thayer came from money . . . like Lauren.

This place is a dump—aside from his vast collection of electronics.

The carpet is stained and matted. The furniture looks like it was found on someone's curb and loaded into the back of his buddy's pickup truck. And it smells like pot ash and weed. All this time, and I never knew Thayer smoked up. Makes me wonder what else I don't know about him.

Or Lauren.

I mean, do we ever truly know anyone or are we only seeing what they want us to see?

Crossing her legs, Lauren's ankle bounces and she nibbles her thumbnail. This isn't like her. Then again, with everything that's transpired in the past week, none of us is really ourselves. Checking her phone, she taps out a text and we sit in palpable silence until the whoosh and hiss of Thayer's shower fills the small apartment.

He's taking his time, and I have half a mind to assume he's doing it out of spite. When he first saw me standing at his door, his eyes flashed dark, his lips pressing flat. He used to be cool with me but now? Since I basically accused him of murder? I'm beginning to think he hates me.

And maybe Lauren knows he hates me and that's why she's so antsy? She knows how he can be sometimes . . . unreasonable and controlling. I'm sure there's a whole world of complexities layered beneath his typical-college-boy facade.

My mind wanders to Elisabeth.

I left a tray of scrambled eggs and buttered toast outside her room along with a note saying I had some business to take care of. I didn't feel right about any of it.

"What's taking him so long?" Lauren sighs, sliding her phone in her left pocket. "Hold on. I'll check."

Sauntering back to his room, I watch her knock and then disappear inside a second later. The door closes quickly.

I don't hear a thing after that.

If they're talking . . . they're whispering.

As soon as the door opens a second later and the two of them emerge and return to the living room, Lauren avoids my gaze.

Thayer's hair is damp, combed, and parted on the side, and he's dressed in jeans and a polo. His thick cologne fills the small space the three of us share.

"Ready?" I ask, standing, my hand gripped around my purse strap. My palms are sweating and my stomach turns.

Lauren and Thayer exchange looks, as they've been doing. But that's what they do. It's what they've always done. It's like they speak their own language. Only right now, I'd love the hell out of an interpreter because something's amiss.

"We should leave now," I say, eyeing the door.

Thayer hooks his hands on his hips, positioning himself so Lauren is blocked from my view. "We've decided not to go."

"What? Why?" I ask.

"None . . . of us . . . is going," he says, taking his time. He reaches for something in his back waistband.

I'm going to be sick.

"You should sit down, Meadow," Lauren says, watching Thayer as if she's waiting for a sign or a signal.

"No." I march toward the door, my back to them and my hand on the knob. "If you guys want to stay here, fine. But I'm going."

It doesn't hit me until now, that I realize I'm stranded. My car is back at campus, where I met Lauren, and the nearest bus stop is a good five-mile walk from here. Either way, I'm leaving. I'll walk to a gas station and call an Uber or whatever.

I just don't want to stay here.

I *can't* stay here.

Every part of me is screaming to get the hell away from these two.

"Sit down, Meadow," Thayer says, his tone dark and laced with power. He rakes his hand across his jaw, and for a second I catch a menacing smirk that disappears in a flash.

When I turn to face them, I find a black handgun pointed in my face. He yanks my purse—which contains my phone—off my shoulder and tosses it into his kitchen. It slams against the wall, contents spilling.

"What the hell are you doing?" I ask. "What is this? Lauren?"

She still won't look at me.

Fucking coward.

Checking her phone, she tells Thayer someone's almost there—two minutes away.

"Good," he says. "We'll just sit tight then. Meadow. Couch. Now."

I don't move. I can't. I'm frozen. Paralyzed.

"Now." He speaks through clenched teeth and his voice booms, startling Lauren.

Stepping carefully, I make my way past the two of them and take a seat at the far end of the couch. Thayer takes the chair across from me and Lauren stands between him and the door, as if I might try to escape with a crazy guy pointing a handgun at me.

When there's a quick rap at the door a minute later, Thayer tells Lauren to get it and she moves as though her life depends on it. Funny, all this time I thought Lauren had the upper hand.

The door swings open and a woman in a black jacket and dark jeans enters, her hair pulled away from her face and tucked under a baseball cap.

Our eyes meet.

"Elisabeth?" I begin to stand until Thayer points his gun in my face again and tells me to "sit the fuck down."

The door slams behind her.

I'm going to be sick.

41

"Meadow?" Elisabeth is surprised to see me.

"You two know each other?" Thayer asks.

"You all know each other?" I answer his question with a question of my own.

"She's my sister," he says.

"*Half* sister," Elisabeth corrects him. The distinction must be important to her. She turns to Lauren while pointing at me. "The girl you described is *nothing* like her. You said she was your fucking mini-me."

"She is," Lauren says. "She basically . . . I don't know . . . became me."

Elisabeth rubs her temple, her winded breath steadying. "Great. This is . . . this is just great."

Thayer hasn't moved an inch, keeping the gun trained in my direction.

"I'm sorry, Meadow." Elisabeth's voice softens, but her face is hard lines and dark circles. "You're a good person. You don't deserve this, and I'm truly sorry. I mean that."

"Sorry for what, Elisabeth?" I say her name and I speak to her as a friend. A friend who has dropped everything to be there for her in her time of need. A friend who has done nothing but listen and cook her food and clean her house and quell her loneliness.

Friends don't kill friends.

But if she's capable of ordering a hit on her husband . . . she's capable of anything.

Thayer sniffs. "Come on, Meadow. You're not that dense. You've been piecing this shit together from the start."

Slight tremors rush over me, electric shocks that come and go. "You set me up. The three of you."

Lauren looks down. Thayer smirks. Elisabeth says nothing.

"You only needed a roommate so you had someone to frame," I speak to Lauren. They had it all planned from the start. They wanted to find some quiet, awkward girl, rope her into their inner circle, plant evidence, then accuse her of being dangerously obsessed.

And it made sense why she kept saying I was perfect . . .

I was a blank canvas, unremarkable and impressionable, and she was planning her masterpiece.

This could've happened to anyone.

I just happened to be the first one to answer the ad. And I was exactly the person they were looking for. Someone socially lost and awkward, someone who needed friends. She saw exactly what I needed before I even knew I needed it—and then she used it against me.

Manipulative bitch.

Everything was a lie from the moment I walked into that house.

Everything.

And that day Thayer was grilling me about who Lauren might be sneaking around with? He was only fishing, only trying to see what I knew at that point. He was never some forlorn lover, some jealous boyfriend. He was only a man on a mission, trying to keep their little plan from falling apart.

"So what now? You're going to shoot me?" My voice wavers, though I'm trying my damnedest to keep a brave face. "You don't think it'll raise any red flags to the police when the roommate of the girl who was sleeping with the professor who was murdered . . . winds up murdered?"

Elisabeth tucks her chin against her chest, pinching the bridge of her nose. "Will one of you explain how this is going to go down. I can't right now. It's like slaughtering your pet chicken so you can eat it for dinner."

"Yeah, we'd hate for you to have murder on your conscience." Thayer speaks under his breath, rolling his eyes. He lowers his gun for a moment. "You know, Meadow, killing you wasn't part of the plan. At all. We had our alibis locked down, our evidence planted. We just wanted the heat on someone else—we didn't even intend for you to be convicted. But you kept digging and digging. And you couldn't keep your mouth shut. And *we* had an agreement. If one of us goes down, we *all* go down. That's why we couldn't let you go to the police about Elisabeth. I mean, hell. You gave us a good scare when you marched down there and told them it was me."

His jaw flexes, eyes squinting.

The police said he had an alibi: his sister.

Of course.

"Lauren, get some paper," Elisabeth says. A moment later I'm being handed a notebook and a pen. "This is your confession. And your final goodbye."

The pen shakes in my hand.

They're staging a suicide.

My suicide.

42

I'm hunched over Thayer's coffee table, my hand trembling so violently I'm not sure I'll be able to write my name, but I don't have a choice.

There's a gun to my head.

And three people who have made it their mission to see to it I die today and take the blame with me.

"Hurry up," Thayer says after a minute.

"I'm trying." My eyes burn, welling with thick, hot tears. "I don't know what to say."

"You're the writer, Elisabeth." He turns to his sister.

She exhales, massaging her temples, before waving her left hand in the air and frowning. "I don't know. Just say you've loved Reed Bristowe but when you found out he was expecting a child and happily married you knew there was no chance with him so . . . you know. Just put it all in your own words—in your own voice. Then end it with an apology and anything else you'd like your family to know."

My lips purse and a fat teardrop falls, staining the lined paper beneath my hand. All this time, I realize Elisabeth never once took an interest in my life. I'd let her vent for hours, rambling on about her work and her husband and her childhood, but never did she ask about mine.

The signs were there all along. Elisabeth Bristowe is as self-centered as they come, a bona fide narcissistic sociopath.

"Come on now." Elisabeth clears her throat, stepping closer. I can't look at her, but I imagine she's staring down at the blank, tearstained page in front of me.

What I wish I could write is that all I wanted was a cheap room to rent. I didn't plan this. I swear.

I'm innocent.

But all eyes are on me.

43

To Whom It May Concern:

I am the sole person responsible for the murder of Meyer State University professor Reed Bristowe.

I was in love with him.

The feelings were not mutual.

I can't bear to live with what I've done, so I've decided to take my own life.

Signed,

Meadow Rain Cupples

44

"Let me see it." Elisabeth yanks the paper out from under me the moment the ink is dry on my signature.

The handwriting is shoddy and barely legible, but I made damn sure my message was void of emotion, undeniably impersonal. If someone murders their "lover" it's normally a crime of passion. If my letter is formal, maybe they'll know it was a setup?

I may be long gone by then, but I'll be damned if these three walk free.

"This is boring as shit." Elisabeth hands it back after studying me for a moment. "But we don't have time for a rewrite."

Thank God.

Taking a couple of steps back, Elisabeth rubs her belly, like it's any other day. Somehow the tenderness is still there, but I don't think someone this evil is capable of love. Not in any genuine, lasting capacity. No wonder she spent her entire college career obsessed with Reed, friendless with no desire to have a social life outside their relationship.

"Was it real? What you had with Reed?" I ask Lauren. Thayer and Elisabeth stare her down. By the looks of it, I'm guessing it was.

"Since you're not going to answer . . ." Elisabeth says, ". . . yes. I walked in on my little brother's girlfriend screwing my husband in the guest room on New Year's Eve last year. And then I found pictures on his phone." She fakes a gag. "The only person in this world that I loved was fucking some student twelve years my junior. My life had become a living, breathing cliché. And he needed to pay. It's as simple as that."

I see it now, the coldness in her eyes. This entire thing was planned out move by move. Intricate with clockwork parts. Strategic—like her novels.

I turn to Thayer. "You and Lauren . . . was that all an act? Since you knew all along?"

Elisabeth answers for him again, "Shockingly, no. And don't even waste your time trying to figure them out. I stopped trying a long time ago. So not worth it."

"I thought we were friends," I say to her. "I was there for you when no one else was."

Her brows meet and she moves toward me. "I know, Meadow. We were. And I'll never forget you and what you've done for me. Truly, you're a gem. And again, I can't tell you how sorry I am about all of this."

Half of me believes her, but only for a split second.

She's a monster. A murderer.

Elisabeth Bristowe is anything but sorry.

I've heard it said before a million times . . . that thing that happens when someone's about to die. Their whole life flashes before their eyes. I always thought it was this tacky way of saying someone was looking back on their life, the good and the bad, their accomplishments and regrets.

But in this moment, the saddest thing isn't that I'm about to die.

It's that I don't have anything to look back on.

I'm twenty-two years old, and I haven't lived at all.

I have no friends. No one to love me or miss me when I'm gone.

I haven't done anything of real significance—nothing to contribute to the greater good in any kind of meaningful way.

When I die, the world won't feel my void.

I've done nothing but hide myself away from the rest of the world, which has done nothing but deny myself of the kind of things I should be thinking about in this moment, seconds from the end of my life.

I want to live.

I'm *going* to live.

"You don't have to do this. If you let me leave, I won't tell a soul. I promise." I lie before accidentally (on purpose) dropping the pen. It rolls beneath the coffee table. Elisabeth's belly is too big for her to bend and if Thayer reaches for it, it means he'll have to lower his gun.

I *might* be able to run then . . .

I'm almost positive Lauren neglected to lock the front door after Elisabeth arrived.

Half of me wishes the smallest part of Lauren feels guilty for this. And I hope it will haunt her the rest of her days. For the rest of her life, I hope she sees my face every time she closes her eyes. I hope she's racked with guilt. I hope it eats her alive, from the inside out. There's not enough makeup in the world to hide an ugly soul.

"If you're not happy with it, maybe let her rewrite it?" Lauren suggests. Her gaze flicks to mine. "It has to be perfect. This is her only chance to say goodbye."

As much as I hate to admit it, for a sliver of my doleful little life, she was my friend. And I was hers. There were moments of our friendship that were rooted in something real and genuine.

"Absolutely not," Elisabeth chuffs. "I want to get this over with. I can't stand her staring at me with that pathetic look on her face."

Pathetic? Try terrified, desperate, hurt.

"Please?" I ask, voice shaking. "I can write a better one. I . . . I was nervous. I still need to write something for my grandmother."

"You're something else, Meadow." Elisabeth eyes the pen on the floor. "Thayer, grab the pen. Get her another piece of paper. You have two minutes."

Just as I hoped it would happen, Thayer drops to the floor, his gun lowered and his arm buried beneath the bottom shelf of the coffee table, searching for the pen I "dropped."

I don't waste a single millisecond.

I bolt.

Pushing past Elisabeth, she loses her balance, screaming for Thayer to grab me, and as he scrambles to get off the floor, my hands are already around the brass doorknob. The cool metal on my palms feels like heaven, and while I can hardly breathe, I promise myself to run like hell the moment I make it outside.

From the corner of my eye, I almost swear I see Lauren taking a step back. While Thayer is reaching, trying to grab me, she's staying out of the way. But I don't have time to think about that, not when I'm quite literally straddling a line between living and dying.

The door sticks at first, but I give it a hard pull and it swings open. With legs ready to sprint down the rickety metal stairs that lead to the parking lot, I burst through the doorway, only to knock into someone.

It takes a second for me to come to, and when I do, I find myself on the concrete walkway outside Thayer's door, back against the handrail. Peering up, the midday sun nearly blinds me after being in that dark lair of an apartment for the past hour, but when I rub my eyes, I focus on an outstretched hand and I let it pull me up.

It's Detective Caldwell.

"Meadow," he says. He looks bulkier than the last time, and I think he might be wearing a Kevlar vest under his button-down shirt. "Get out of here. Go. *Now*."

Before I have a chance to comprehend any of this, a uniformed police officer is escorting me down the stairway and leading me to a covered section of the building, out of sight.

45

Despite the fact that I'm safe and sound, wrapped in a thick, woolen blanket and surrounded by painted cinder block walls and an entire department of law enforcement officers, I can't stop shaking.

I'm free.

They placed me in Caldwell's office and sent some woman in to determine if I needed a referral for a victim liaison counselor. It took a lot of insisting, but finally they were able to see that I'm fine.

I have nowhere to go after this . . . but at least I'm alive.

The oversized clock on Caldwell's wall has one of those smooth second hands, the kind that don't tick, and there's a baseball-shaped stress ball next to his phone. There's nothing to do here. I don't have my phone or my bag or my car keys—everything is in Thayer's apartment, scattered on his kitchen floor where he threw them.

My chair is hard and my lower back is beginning to ache, so I swap it out for Caldwell's and push his up to the wall. Repositioning my blanket and wrapping it around me, I close my eyes and try to rest. I'm not tired—far from it—but these fluorescent lights are giving me a headache.

I'm not sure how much time has passed when his door swings open and I'm startled into the present moment.

"You hungry?" Lee has a white paper sack in his hands and a Styrofoam cup. "Wasn't sure what you liked, so I got you a burger and fries and a chocolate shake."

I let the blanket fall around my shoulders and wheel myself to his desk.

"It's a comfortable chair, isn't it?" he asks.

"You want it back?" I unwrap the burger and shove a fry in my mouth, hating that the scent of greasy food makes me homesick in the weirdest way. Growing up, Mom never cooked. We ate McDonald's every Monday, Thursday, and Friday—her late work days—and when she'd waitress on the weekends, she'd always come home smelling like a deep-fat fryer.

We don't get to decide what home means, I guess.

"Nah," he says, watching me inhale this food.

"Thank you for this." I take a sip of the shake, and the thick, icy liquid soothes my hot, dry throat and gifts my belly with a comforting fullness. "So where are they?"

He knows exactly to whom I'm referring.

"In custody," he says without missing a beat. "Has anyone . . . filled you in yet? On everything?"

Setting the cup aside, I look him square in the eyes. "Nope."

His chin juts forward and he nods. "Okay . . ."

I shove my food aside, shut my mouth, and listen as he fills me in on everything.

And when he's finished, he tells me the only reason I'm here right now, breathing this stale office air . . . is because of Lauren Wiedenfeld.

She saved my life.

"I want to see her," I say to him when he's finished.

His nose wrinkles, like I'm asking an impossible favor.

"I want to see her," I repeat, clearer this time.

"Meadow, I don't know if that's a good idea." He sounds apologetic but doesn't look it. "She's a suspect and you're a victim. Even if I wanted to, it's against—"

"Please." I stand. I'm not taking no for an answer. Not after everything I've been through today.

His lips press together and he releases a hard breath.

"Detective Caldwell, I just want to talk to her. She saved my life," I say. "I just want to ask her one question and I'll be on my way." He drags his hand through his hair, hesitating. "You can supervise. You can stand there the entire time."

I shove the fast food dinner aside and fold my arms before glancing toward the door.

It takes him a moment, but he finally stands. "I'll give you one minute with her. That's it."

"That's all I need."

Caldwell leads me down a series of hallways until we reach a small room with a two-way window. Scanning his badge, the lock on the door gives a clunky release and he escorts me in.

Lauren, in all her former perfection, is seated at a table, dressed in orange. Her ankles secured together and her hands cuffed. Blonde hair hangs in her face and her shoulders slump. It takes her a second to realize it's me standing before her.

"Meadow," she says, eyes wide.

Half of me wants to scream in her face.

The other half of me wants to thank her.

I hate that she's put me in this position . . . I hate that she's lowered me to the point of feeling guilt over the way I feel about the very person who put my life in danger.

"I just have one question." My arms tighten across my chest, my head cocks to the side. I wait for her bloodshot eyes to find mine. "Was it ever real for you?"

She licks her lips, glancing down at her cuffed, manicured hands, their warm, creamy color a stark clash against the cool metal. Lauren knows exactly what I'm asking.

I want to know if we were ever friends.

Maybe it's a moot point. Maybe it's one of those questions that are better left unanswered, but I have to know. The question burns inside of me, intense and nagging. It will not be ignored.

"Almost," she says after a moment, exhaling.

I was hoping for a "yes." I would've been okay with a "no." I wasn't prepared for an "almost."

My eyes burn, but I blink away the tears before anyone notices.

We were almost friends—almost.

"You're a shitty human being," I say.

Caldwell clears his throat.

"I know." Lauren's voice is barely audible, slightly strained.

"But thank you for saving me," I say.

She says nothing, as if the simple formality of "you're welcome" feels inappropriate in this moment.

And it is.

Lauren Wiedenfeld may have saved the day, but she's no hero.

I turn to Caldwell. "Get me out of here."

If I never see my roommate again, it will be too soon.

46

My mom won't stop staring from across her kitchen table. Caldwell called her to come get me tonight and for the first time in history, she dropped everything and came to my rescue. It probably helped that he told her I was nearly shot and killed . . .

"I never want to get a call like that again," she breaks her silence, and for a moment, it sounds like she's blaming *me* for this. I've only been home for an hour and already we're going there? "If anyone ever tries to hurt you again, Meadow, so help me . . ."

Oh.

She's . . . *defending* me?

This . . .

This is new.

Her bleached blonde hair is pulled into a tight ponytail, the dark roots greasy. She looks as if she just finished working a double, her eyes baggy and bloodshot. I'm positive she'd rather be in bed, in the room with the tinfoil-covered windows and the noisy box fan perched on her dresser.

The corner by the fridge, where Bug used to keep an open bag of store-brand dog food for his Doberman . . . is empty. Swept out. And come to think of it, the place smells a little less . . . musty.

"Where's Bug?" I ask.

"Kicked him out a few weeks ago." She shakes her head. "He met some other woman online, some gamer. Son of a bitch wanted his cake and thought he could eat it, too."

Mom may have belowground standards when it comes to men, but she's always drawn the line at cheating.

Good riddance.

"I stole some coins from him." I pick at a hangnail on my right thumb, tearing at it until it bleeds, but I don't feel a thing. If there's ever going to be an opportune moment to share this, it's now, while she's calling him a "son of a bitch."

"I know."

I glance up. "You do?"

She nods. "I'd been tapping into that myself from time to time. The dumbass had no idea they were worth anything. Thought they were just some stupid pennies his grandpa had been collecting for years. Anyway, I knew you'd taken them after the last time you stopped by. Didn't want to make it into a thing because, well, you know . . . Bug and his temper. Idiot didn't even notice the box missing when he was loading up his shit. I'm not worried."

Exhaling, I lean back in my chair. I'm not proud of what I did, and I justified it six ways from Sunday, but I take comfort for the time being, knowing the potbellied dipshit won't be coming after me with a loaded shotgun.

"Why'd you take the gun, Meadow?" Mom asks. "He was pretty upset about that . . . just 'cause he didn't want anyone to get hurt."

Brows lifted, I smirk at the thought of Bug worrying about anyone's safety. I'm guessing he cared more about the liability factor than anyone getting hurt.

"I hate guns," I say. "And I hate Bug. Just wanted to throw it into the lake."

"Anyway, you going to fill me in on everything?" she asks, leaving the table and heading for the cupboard by the sink. Mom retrieves two chipped mugs we've had since the beginning of time, and then she fills them with water from the tap before placing them in the little countertop microwave. She closes the door, presses a button, and a gentle hum fills the kitchen. "You were so quiet on the ride home. Thought maybe you needed some time to decompress, but I won't be able to sleep tonight until I know why the hell someone would want to *kill* my daughter. You've never done a damn thing to anybody, Meadow. You're a good kid, even if I can't take credit for it. I don't understand why someone would want to hurt you."

Gathering my thoughts, I take a deep breath as the microwave beeps a minute later. Mom pulls a tin of powdered cappuccino mix from a different cupboard before grabbing a tablespoon from the silverware drawer.

It isn't Earl Grey or organic green tea and it's probably a couple of years old. And I feel like most mothers usually know if their daughters like coffee or not . . . but at least this is something.

It's a start.

A baby step in the right direction.

"So, tell me, Meadow," Mom says, yawning. "Why'd these assholes do this to you?"

I start from the beginning. The eviction. The want ad. 47 Magpie Drive. The clothes. The hair. The friends. The coins. The car. The attention. The special treatment. The secret affair. The lies upon lies upon lies. The murder. The forced suicide that almost happened.

And then I tell her about the girl at the center of it all.

Lauren. My *perfect* roommate, who at zero hour, grew a conscience and silently sent a text message to Caldwell while Thayer had his gun pointed at my head and Elisabeth was yelling for me to hurry up and write my "confession."

She also had the forethought to record the audio. The *entire* thing.

Apparently, Elisabeth and Thayer were blackmailing her, threatening to anonymously disseminate the nude photos and videos she'd texted to Reed, posting them on adult websites and the dark web where they'd be reproduced and shared at warp speed, multiplying at an impossible rate. They'd be out there, forever, for anyone to see for the rest of her life. Lauren was terrified.

From the sound of it, they used her as bait in their little scheme. And by the time they admitted they planned on actually killing Bristowe (as they first told her it was simply a kidnap-for-ransom deal and no one would get hurt), she was already in too deep. They could turn on her just as easy as she could turn on them . . . and they wouldn't have hesitated. She did what she thought she had to do.

Not that I'm defending her.

Caldwell says he'll keep me posted, and the local news affiliates are already on it, sending their field correspondents to the Meyer State campus in search of sound bites. So far everyone's in shock and disbelief. And one very stoned student called the whole thing "cray cray" on live TV.

"You look tired," Mom says, placing my powdered cappuccino drink in front of me.

"So do you."

"Your eyes twitch when you're sleepy." She smiles, drinking me in like she's seeing me—really seeing me—for the first time in ages.

"So do yours." I take a sip of my coffee, a small sip, and try to ignore the cheap taste on my tongue.

"Everything's going to be okay, Meadow," she says a moment later. "You know how I know that?"

"How?"

"Because you're my daughter. And we're strong," she says. "We stand up for what we want and what we believe in and right or wrong, we don't let anybody else control our compass." She takes the seat beside me, overworked hands cupping her mug. I can't remember the last time we sat, just the two of us, and talked about anything. This very well may be the first time. "We're more alike than we're different. And sooner or later we all turn into our mothers."

"But you're nothing like Grandma." I think of my grandmother's overfilled porcelain doll curio cabinet, doily-covered coffee tables, immaculate 1980s-era kitchen, and her home-cooked Sunday dinners.

"You don't know the woman I grew up with." Eyes rolling, she cups her pointed chin in her hand. "God, we fought like cats and dogs. She kicked me out about half a dozen times and I ran away a half a dozen other times. But you know what? She always left the back door unlocked and I always came back."

Mom yawns again. I yawn, too.

I think this is her way of saying Grandma was always there for her and she's always going to be there for me? But I'm not entirely sure. She's never been good at apologies or expressing feelings that run deeper than surface level, and I suspect for the time being, this is about as momentous as it's going to get.

"Your room is empty. We'll need to get you a new bed, but you can have mine tonight. I'll take the couch," she says.

"You don't have to do that—" I have no intentions of staying here longer than a day or two. Not sure where I'm going next, but I can't stay here and tread these same old waters.

"Don't argue with me." She rises, one hand on her hip like she doesn't have time for this shit.

There's the Misty Cupples I know.

Obviously, I don't know what it's like to be a mother, but I imagine the threat of losing your only child might rearrange your priorities or gift you with the kind of perspective you didn't have before.

Only time will tell.

"Good night, Meadow," she says before shuffling away in the flattened and faded house slippers I gave her eight Christmases ago. "Get some sleep."

47

Two Months Later . . .

"Meadow." Someone calls my name from a sea of graduates dressed in shiny purple robes. "Over here."

Scanning the crowd, my gaze settles on a dark-haired girl offering a hesitant wave, her familiar round eyes trained on me.

"Tessa." I amble toward her, equally as reluctant, my heels sinking into the grass.

I haven't seen her since . . . before.

"How have you been?" Her graduation tassel hangs in her face, and she moves it aside. "I've been meaning to get a hold of you . . ."

Tessa's explanation dwindles, but I don't hold it against her. I could hardly expect her to know what to say in regards to a situation like this. And besides, I'm not sure we were ever really more than acquaintances sharing a common friend. Sure, we hung out from time to time, but we didn't have the kind of strong bond I once thought I shared with Lauren.

But we did have our moments.

"It's okay," I say, offering an understated smile. "This last month has been . . . crazy."

She exhales, glancing down, nodding. "That's putting it nicely."

Detective Caldwell informed me weeks ago that they'd brought Tessa in for questioning, that she knew nothing. During the process, she also inadvertently offered a few missing pieces of the puzzle, which was a relief. I'm not sure I could've handled one more betrayal.

That night my location data was cleared out of my phone? Tessa had seen Thayer going through it. She didn't think anything of it at the time, assuming I'd given it to him to take a picture or fix a setting. When Caldwell questioned Lauren about it, she admitted Thayer drove us past the Bristowes' on the way home from the bar that evening so their address would register on my app, trying to make it look like I was stalking them. That story about me going home with some guy? A complete fabrication. After she and Thayer carried me to my bed and he left, she meant to take a screenshot of my location history but accidentally deleted everything.

That's why everything prior to three AM was gone.

Anyway, Thayer hasn't admitted to any of this. He and Elisabeth can hardly afford a decent lawyer from what I hear. All the Bristowe assets are frozen. Their futures are in the hands of a fresh-out-of-law-school public defender.

And that poor baby girl. Elisabeth will be giving birth in a prison hospital soon. I imagine if some next of kin doesn't step up, she'll be fostered out. Hopefully to a nice, *normal* family—if those even exist anymore.

"I'm still trying to wrap my head around everything. Still doesn't feel real," Tessa says, chewing the inside of her lower lip. "You think you know people . . ."

Licking my lips, I press them together, contemplating what I should say. It never occurred to me until just now that she's feeling just as betrayed by all of this—maybe to a lesser extent—but still.

They lied to us both.

And in their own ways, they used us both.

"Have you talked to Lauren at all?" I ask, purely out of curiosity.

"Nope." Tessa glances down, pausing. "Heard she was offered a plea deal and she took it. My guess is she's holed up at her parents' house in Albany. Hiding."

Coward.

"So she won't be going to jail?" My jaw is about to drop before Tessa starts shaking her head.

"No, she will. Just not as long as the other two," she says. "So, what are you doing after this?"

For a moment, I'm positive she's asking if I want to hang out. Tessa never really had a lot of close friends outside of Lauren, only a few girls she'd meet up with at the bar. No one she'd ever take the time to have lunch with or text when she's bored.

I shrug, eyeing my mom from across the open field. She's standing by herself, nose buried in her phone. It means a lot that she even came. I honestly didn't expect her to. But she's been doing that lately—defying my expectations and surprising me. I think she's trying.

"Going home." I lift a brow. "You?"

Tessa laughs. "No, I mean. Did you find a job? Are you leaving Monarch Falls?"

"Oh." I chuckle. "Yeah. I found a job in Chicago. Moving in a couple weeks. What about you?"

"Going back to South Dakota," she says. "I miss my family."

Tessa points to an older man and woman standing, his arm around her shoulders. They're chatting with two guys who appear to be around Tessa's age. They all share the same shiny dark hair and honey eyes. One of the guys laugh. The dad slugs his shoulder. Her mom glances up with this sweet, still-in-love-after-all-these-years kind of look on her face.

There's a tightness in my chest . . . somewhere between being happy for Tessa's seemingly "normal" family and becoming hopelessly consumed by an irrational wave of stark raving jealousy.

Pulling in a sharp breath, I remind myself there's no such thing as normal.

Or perfect.

Especially not perfect.

"Meadow, you ready?" Mom appears from behind me, checking the time on her phone. "Have to be to work by seven. Need to get going."

"Yep," I say to Mom, before giving Tessa a quick smile. "Good luck with everything."

"You too." She lingers for a moment. "Keep in touch?"

The idea of staying in touch with Tessa doesn't fill me with warm fuzzies or preemptive nostalgia. In fact, leaving Monarch Falls and all of its inhabitants—past and present—is the only thing that remotely fills me with the kind of thing that puts a dopey little smile on my face.

All I want to do is live. *Truly* live.

And I can't do that here. This place is marred and tainted and ugly, and it's time to close this chapter of my life for good.

"Bye, Tessa." With that, I walk away, disappearing into the sea of purple, shedding my cap and gown and tossing them into a nearby trash can.

Epilogue

Six Months Later

"As soon as my towels are done, the dryer's all yours." Her name is Bethany Nielsen. "Do you want to get lunch in a bit?" And she's my roommate. "I'm thinking sushi?"

I give her a bug-eyed stare.

"Kidding." She laughs, tucking her silky, chocolate-brown hair behind her ears. "I know you hate sushi. I don't care where we go, I'm just starving."

When I left Monarch Falls on a Greyhound bus headed for Chicago, all my belongings in two giant suitcases, I promised myself no roommates.

But living in Chicago isn't cheap, and the "generous" salary I was offered doing insurance submissions for a private practice in the Lincoln Park neighborhood doesn't stretch as far as I thought it would. Maybe it was naive of me to take this job and make this impulsive move and not give it much thought, but at the time I was desperate to be anywhere but there. And now that I'm here, I can't imagine being anywhere else.

Chicago is the exact opposite of Monarch Falls, which means it's hustle and bustle. Culture galore. Great shopping and even better food.

Two-point-seven million people out here living their best lives. The excitement is contagious, powerful enough to pull my homebody self out of my ironclad shell.

But I wasn't here long before I found myself sitting up in my apartment most nights, eating ramen and cold cereal and binge-watching mediocre TV shows. The old me may have been content to live like that, but the new me refused.

When I contacted the landlord last month to see if there were any cheaper units available I could move to, he told me he had a tenant looking to sublet one of her rooms. He stressed to me that they normally didn't allow this, but it was his niece and he was making an exception as a favor to her parents.

"If you're not hungry, that's cool," Bethany says, taking the spot beside me on her sofa. She's got this mid-century modern kind of vibe going on in here. Clean lines, zero clutter, and mixed metal accents. She's completely obsessed with *Mad Men* and anything vintage. Her bedroom looks like a page out of a 1958 issue of *Good Housekeeping* and her closet is stocked with enviable, hard-to-find pieces from eras past. I'm convinced her entire life could be filmed with a Super 8 camera and no one would question its authenticity.

"No, I'll go." I pause the episode of *Mad Men* playing on the TV. She convinced me to start watching it last week. Now I'm three seasons in and hooked like a fish. "Is Monteverde in the West Loop okay? I've been craving their gnocchetti."

"You had me at Monteverde." Bethany twists her fingers around the string of pearls hanging around her neck and then grins. She's quirky and fun. Nothing like Lauren. What you see is what you get with her—at least from what I can tell. She works as an art teacher in a local public school and her personality is simply infectious. Everybody loves her and with good reason. She's always happy, smiling.

I'm lucky to call her my friend.

Rising, I head to my room to freshen up, first slicking on two coats of the matte "Betty Draper Red" lipstick Bethany recommended for me the other week. When I'm done, I check my reflection in the mirror, smoothing the creases of the floral, tea-length dress we found at a vintage thrift shop yesterday. Slipping the matching Jackie O–style coat over my shoulders, I fasten the button at the top and give myself a final once-over before running my hands along the shiny blonde curls that stop just above my jawline.

I'm missing something . . .

Fishing around in my jewelry box, I retrieve a pearl necklace just like my roommate's and fasten it around my neck.

There. Now I'm perfect.

Acknowledgments

This book would not have been possible if it weren't for the following incredibly talented and passionate souls.

Louisa Maggio, thank you for the original gorgeous cover. Your talent is second to none.

Wendy Chan, your eagle eyes and timeliness are a godsend. Thanks for always squeezing me in and working with my insane deadlines!

To my betas, Ashley Cestra, Pamela Hull, Deanna Finn, Jacqueline Scifres, and Shannon Casey, this book would not be what it is if it weren't for your invaluable feedback. Thank you so much for taking time out of your busy schedules to read and critique for me.

To my ARC readers, social media followers, fans, and all those who have showered me with kindness, encouragement, and support since *The Memory Watcher* released, your messages and emails have not gone unnoticed. It's been a wild ride, and I hope you're buckled in tight!

About the Author

Photo © 2024 Jill Austin Photography

Minka Kent is the *Washington Post* and *Wall Street Journal* bestselling author of *After Dark, The Watcher Girl, When I Was You, The Stillwater Girls, The Thinnest Air, The Perfect Roommate, The Memory Watcher, Unmissing, The Silent Woman, Gone Again, People Like Them, After Dark,* and *Imaginary Strangers.* Her work has been featured in *People* magazine and the *New York Post* as well as optioned for film and TV. Minka also writes contemporary romance as *Wall Street Journal* and #1 Amazon Charts bestselling author Winter Renshaw. She is a graduate of Iowa State University and resides in Iowa with her three children. For more information, visit http://minkakent.com.